HARD LAND
COLORADO TERRITORY BOOK VI

JOHN LEGG

WOLFPACK
PUBLISHING
— EST 2013 —

Hard Land
Paperback Edition
Copyright © 2022 John Legg

Wolfpack Publishing
9850 S. Maryland Parkway, Suite A-5 #323
Las Vegas, Nevada 89183

wolfpackpublishing.com

Paperback ISBN 978-1-63977-447-0
eBook ISBN 978-1-63977-446-3
LCCN 2022947821

HARD LAND

CHAPTER ONE

It was with a deep-seated sense of dread that Brodie Pike rode into Many Snows's village. The old chief did not come out of his lodge, but Blind Bull and Crazy Hawk waited. The Utes' smiles of greeting quickly turned to frowns when they realized Pike was alone.

Without a word, Blind Bull and Crazy Hawk slipped into the former's lodge.

Pike dismounted and handed the reins of his horse and mule to a teenager, ducked into the tipi, and took a seat at the fire. "Where's Many Snows?" Pike asked.

"In the beyond." Not waiting for Pike to finish eating the roasted elk Blind Bull's oldest wife had handed him, the older warrior asked, "Where is Little Raven?"

"Gone under."

"How?" the younger Ute asked, reaching for his knife.

"You try pullin' that blade, Hawk, and you'll be dead before it clears the sheath."

Glaring at Pike, Crazy Hawk moved his hand away from the weapon's hilt.

"Why're you concerned, Hawk? You didn't much give a damn when she was alive."

"Any time we lose one of us it saddens us," Blind Bull said solemnly.

"It saddens me too. Very much," the white man responded.

Blind Bull nodded. "What happened?"

"When we left here, we wandered up north, with no place in particular in mind. For two years me and Little Raven traveled through the Sangre de Cristos. That first winter we found us a cave where we settled in. In the spring I left her there and went into a new town called Colorado Springs." Pike ignored Crazy Hawk's look of anger. "I picked up some supplies and then did some prospectin', with my woman at my side. I only found a little gold, not that I tried real hard. I ain't much for pannin'. Not enough to settle down on—not that there were many places we could've done so—but enough to get more supplies to move on and try my luck elsewhere. We kept movin' around, doin' a little prospectin', some chasin' outlaws, until winter was closin' in. She was with child, and I offered to bring her back here so she'd have help when birthin' time came, but she refused. Said she'd be fine, and we could come back here in the spring."

"You should've brought her by force if she gave you a hard time," Crazy Hawk said.

"True. And I could've shot you when we first met, and I didn't. Now I regret not having done both."

A wisp of a smile crossed Blind Bull's lips.

"So I finally found us a small, nice valley where we could winter. I left her there like I did last time and went to Colorado Springs and managed to get us enough supplies for winter, and we settled in. She was gathering firewood and I was butcherin' a deer when we were attacked."

"Damn white-eyes," Crazy Hawk snapped.

"She caught two arrows and I was hit once. She died, I didn't." His voice was bitter and angry. "I don't know how many there were, but I wounded a couple of 'em before they took off."

"Damn Shoshonis," Crazy Hawk spat.

Pike looked from him to Blind Bull. "It was Utes."

"You lie!" the younger warrior hissed.

"I been shot at and shot by enough Ute arrows to be able to tell 'em. Besides, I couldn't shoot 'em if I didn't at least catch glimpses of 'em when I was fightin' 'em." He paused as he let the anger and sense of loss settle down some. "I buried her there. I reckon it wasn't the way you would've taken care of her, but I did it the way my people would, as best I could anyway. I still think she's with the Great Spirit in a pleasant afterlife." He paused, wondering if he should say more but decided not to.

Blind Bull nodded. "It is good what you have done. But now we must grieve."

"I understand. I've grieved. In fact, I'm still mournin' my woman. She was as good a woman as a man could have." He smiled crookedly. "Even though she had a mighty sharp tongue at times." He set down the coffee mug. "I'll be leavin' to let you grieve in peace."

"You'll come back?" the older warrior asked.

"I doubt it. No reason to, I reckon." He looked directly at Blind Bull. "You're the only friend I got here." He ignored Crazy Hawk's shocked look. "And I reckon me being here at any time won't sit well with your people."

"They will…"

"They've only accepted me because of you and your daughter."

"You forget me," the younger warrior said, notes of anger and hurt in his voice.

"No, I ain't forgot you, Hawk. I'm just ignorin' you. I don't take kindly to being called a liar, something a friend would never do." He looked back at the older Ute. "Goodbye, Blind Bull. I was proud to be your son-in-law. I wish you and your people well."

"And you, my friend," the warrior said.

Pike pushed out of the lodge and went to his horse which along with the mule was cropping grass behind the tipi. He was tightening the cinch on his saddle when Crazy Hawk walked up.

"I'm sorry I called you a liar," the Ute said. He looked as if he had just swallowed something foul, and Pike knew it was killing the warrior to apologize, especially to him.

"It's over and done."

"We've been through a lot together, Brodie. I saved your life when Red Scar shot you."

"It was your sister who saved me."

Crazy Hawk shrugged. "If I hadn't ridden all night to get her, you wouldn't have made it. I ain't saying that to mean you owe me anything. Just one thing we've gone through together. And you saved my life." A small grin appeared and quickly vanished.

"How'd I do that?"

"By not killing me the dozen or so times you could've." He sighed. "Dammit, Brodie, you know what a damn fool hothead I am. I too often say or do something reckless before my head tells me it's stupid."

"Well, that's something we can agree on."

"We've been friends through other damn fool things I've said or done. I'm asking you to"—he almost choked on what he was about to say—"for..."

Pike slapped a hand on the Ute's shoulder. "It's forgotten, my friend. Take care of your pa and your people. They need a strong warrior, not a foolish, hotheaded one. Hard times are coming for your people. You'll need to lead 'em."

Crazy Hawk nodded. "I'd like you to visit now and again."

"Like I said, I doubt it, but I won't say I won't, or I will. It ain't likely but it's possible."

"Stay in my lodge tonight. It's late for travelin'."

"No, Hawk. You and your father and others need to start your grievin', and I'd only get in the way." He mounted his horse and held out his hand.

"Bye, Brodie," Crazy Hawk said, his voice tinged with sadness.

"Bye, Hawk." Pike took the rope to his mule and rode off without another look back. He knew that he'd never return. He had caused these people trouble and heartache. It was always this way for him—trying to do right but in the end causing trouble for those he tried to help. He wouldn't bring them more.

An hour later, Pike was sure someone was following him, and he shook his head in irritation. He kept riding, though, as dusk began to fall. He pulled off the trail in a spot among the aspens with good grass and a small stream. It would make a good camp. As he tended the animals, he kept his ears on the trail. Finished with that, he gathered wood but did not start a fire yet. Before long, he heard a horse coming. He took a position behind a slim aspen, rifle cocked and ready.

"Stop right there, Hawk," he said. "Go on back to the village. You keep followin' me and there'll be one less warrior in the village and Blind Bull will be grievin' two people."

"You're not gonna shoot me, Brodie," Crazy Hawk said with confidence. "Besides, I got fresh elk to share."

"I could shoot you and take the elk."

"If you were going to do that you already would have. Now, put your rifle away and let's have us a feast."

Pike shook his head both in annoyance and at the Ute's audacity, especially since both feelings were true. "All right, dammit, come ahead."

While Crazy Hawk tended his pony, Pike started a fire and got coffee going. The Ute tossed Pike a hide-wrapped hunk of elk. The white man sliced off two good-sized pieces and got them to roasting on green sticks propped up by rocks. Then the two men sat silently and waited for the meat and coffee to be ready.

When they had finished eating and were on their second cup of coffee, Pike asked, "So what're you doing followin' me? I thought you were grievin'."

"I am. But I realized after you left that I hadn't finished talkin' to you."

"We're talked out, my friend. Ain't anything more to say."

"Yes, there is." The Ute sat staring into the fire, then said quietly, "I know how you feel, Brodie."

"About what?"

"About you thinkin' you've been a curse on my people."

"I have been, and you have no idea how I feel."

"I can't feel what you feel, of course, but I understand havin' the feelin'."

"Good for you."

"I'm here to tell you such a feelin' is nonsense."

Pike looked at him as if he thought the Indian had lost his reason. "You're *loco*, Hawk."

"No, I ain't. You've been a good friend to the Ute, to my people, to my band."

"I am, huh? If it weren't for me, Fallen Timber and all his clan would be alive. Little Winter Sky would be..." He stopped, choking back tears at the thought of the horrifically abused eleven-year-old. "She'd be... if it weren't for me. Dammit, Hawk, if it weren't for me that girl would be getting to an age when boys would be coming 'round her lodge lookin' to make her his wife. It's my fault not only that she's dead but that she was abused, and her parents and all the others are dead."

"And if it weren't for you, their spirits would never be free. We never would have avenged their deaths." Crazy Hawk ignored the fact that Pike was naming dead people, which was not usually done. He would ignore his own use of that taboo.

"Only reason I got revenge for them is because I had brought the trouble on them in the first place." He sighed raggedly. "And now Little Raven is gone. I should have made her stay here in the first place and left."

"I heard how you tried to talk her into letting you leave this land. Didn't work. Didn't work later when you decided to leave the village. Brodie, Fallen Timber's people weren't killed because you're cursed. They're dead because a bunch of white-eye bastards attacked their village and killed them. Winter Sky wasn't abused because you're a bad man for the people. She's dead because some devils with white skin did unimaginable things to her. And Little Raven ain't dead because you're an evil man. She's dead because some damned Utes killed her." He fought to keep down the anger at the fact that her own people had killed Pike's woman.

"I should've forced her to stay in the village."

"My sister was as hardheaded as I am. She would've followed you, no matter how you tried to stop her. You were her man and she belonged at your side. That's how she felt and believed. If you had snuck out of the village, she would've followed, no matter how hard you tried to hide your trail. She would've searched until she found you, or until she died."

"Maybe that's true. But if I hadn't saved Fallen Timber and Light Elk, those men wouldn't have raided the village."

"Those men—or others just like them—would've attacked that village if they found it. You not only gave Fallen Timber a few extra months of life, you gave him back his respect. I won't say he died a happy death, but he did die a proud death."

"Bah."

"I don't know of anybody in my village who blames you for any of this. You've been a friend to the people, and you should remember that."

"Go to hell, Hawk. You're *loco* if you believe any of that rubbish."

"We don't have a hell. Not like yours. If we did, I'd be headed there. And I'll tell you this, Blind Bull and I are grievin' for my sister, his daughter. But we're also grievin' for the loss of our great friend."

Pike looked at him in shock.

"Yes, you, Brodie, you damn fool."

When Pike awoke in the morning Crazy Hawk was gone, but he had left a beautifully decorated sheath, one Pike knew had been made by Little Raven for her brother.

CHAPTER TWO

Pike sat on the hill and looked out over the meadow. He remembered the first time he had seen it, from this very spot, and thought it would be the place to live away from people for a while.

The adobe house he had built by himself was in even worse shape than it had been when he had set off some dynamite inside, blasting the roof in and the walls partly out. Now the elements were well on their way to reclaiming the area and erasing any evidence that a man once lived here. He figured that in another year all trace of him would be gone. A good thing, he figured.

He was rather surprised. After he had fended off an attack by men from Skeeter Creek and sent the survivors packing, he had destroyed the place. He had thought someone from Skeeter Creek would have claimed the place, staking a homestead claim on the beautiful meadow, maybe for farming or, more likely, ranching.

After doing what damage he could to the place, he had planned to leave the area forever, but Little Raven had stopped him and convinced him to live with her in her village. That had lasted only through the winter. By then he was restless and needed to move on. Despite his pain at her death, he had to smile at the remembrance of the time he told her he was leaving. It was a replay of when he was ready to leave the cabin the previous fall.

* * *

"I'll be ready," Little Raven had said when he told her he'd be leaving in the morning.

"You're not going," Pike had insisted.

"Yep. I am."

"You can't. I told you why the last time we had this argument."

"I not argue. You argue. I just say what I say."

"But there'll be times I have to leave you alone while I go into a town or something."

"I work when you gone. Make clothes or moccasins. Make jerky or pemmican."

"No, dammit. I'd worry about you too much if I had to leave you alone. You'd be in big trouble if some other tribe found you. Or, worse, if some white men did."

"I hide. I will be fine. Yep."

"You are the stubbornest damn woman I've ever had the displeasure of meeting."

"Yep." She grinned. Then she grew more serious. She reached out a hand and stroked his stubbled cheek. "I stay if you not want me anymore." When he said nothing but looked pained, she continued. "I say last time, you're my man; I'm your woman. I go where you go. If you hurt, I hurt; if I hurt, you hurt. We have each other."

"But you won't have any friends. You'll be all alone."

"Nope. I have you."

"Ain't the same as having some of your women friends to help you, to talk with."

"That will make me sad, but I will have you."

"You're a damn fool, you know that, woman?"

"Nope. I love my man. He loves me."

The last was more of a question. She smiled when he nodded ever so slightly.

"It's because I love you that I don't want to take you with me. It's too dangerous, and I'd sure be sad if something happened to you. And what'll you do if I die?"

"I worry about that if it happens. I can find way back here."

"Tell you what, you stay here where you're safe and I'll come back every few months to visit."

"You lie."

Pike sighed, frustrated. He did want her along, but the problems of taking her were too much to ignore. Then he considered leaving during the night. That might work, he figured.

He thought she must have read his thought because she said, "If you sneak away, I follow, like I say last time. I go where you go."

"Maybe I'll just tie you up and go."

"You won't do."

Like last time, he knew he had lost the battle. "All right, dammit," he said with a resigned sigh.

For two years he and his Ute woman wandered. At times he would leave her and ride into a town, get a few wanted posters and chase outlaws. Little Raven would ride along with him, at least until the time came for Pike to capture or kill the outlaw. He would leave her again when he brought the miscreant—or his body—into town and collect his reward. Each time he left her, he worried, fear of what might happen to her clutching at him. His excursions to towns were quick and short.

* * *

He considered riding to Skeeter Creek. He didn't think anyone would remember him, and it would be interesting to see if it was still booming or had gone bust and was now a ghost town. But the place would, he decided, bring back too many bad memories—the sight of a small Ute village destroyed, the people killed and mutilated, the sight of an eleven-year-old girl abused beyond anything Pike thought humans could do, the icy pain in his heart when he had to end the girl's suffering, and the pain of knowing that he was, in a way, responsible.

No, he decided, better to stay clear of Skeeter Creek. The devils who had caused all that were gone, dead at Pike's hand, but just the name of the place might be enough to set him off again if he went there. He rode on, sadness riding on his shoulders like a lice-riddled blanket.

CHAPTER THREE

Pike wondered if he would ever get over the loss of Little Raven. Too many times, he would shoot a deer or elk and head back to his small camp, calling out, "Look what I caught, Raven." And the reality of her loss would hit him again, worming its way into his guts. Fresh elk would lose all interest for him when that happened.

A few months after he had left Blind Bull's village, when he had told the warrior and his son, Crazy Hawk, about his daughter's death, he decided that as much danger as he could be to his fellow citizens, it was time to visit a town. And it would be the biggest city he could find. That way he could sample some of the city's pleasures but still remain anonymous. He turned his horse toward Denver.

As he rode into the city he was surprised at its size and activity. He hadn't seen a place this big and bustling since shortly after mustering out after the war a few years ago. He spotted three livery stables and suspected there might be more. For some unfathomable reason, one looked better to him than the others. He pulled in. As he was paying, he asked the liveryman, "Know of a good hotel, restaurant, and... parlor house?"

The stable owner, Bart Blakely, grinned. "Several hotels're fine. You'll find 'em on Larimer Street, same with restaurants. As for the other, well, McGaa Street is the place to go." He peered around in an exaggerated manner as if checking to make sure no one was listening, then added, "Clarissa's is best. Expensive, though."

"Clarissa's, you said?"

"Yep. Know of it?"

"Doubt it. Knew of a place run by a woman named Clarissa in a minin' town southwest of here."

"Look for the place with the red door."

"I will, thanks."

"Sure thing."

Pike grabbed his saddlebags, Henry rifle, and the specially made scabbard holding the .52-caliber Sharps sniper rifle he had used in the Civil War. Hauling them all, he headed toward Larimer Street and found what seemed to be a decent hotel and checked in.

A decent meal, a bath, shave, and haircut, plus a new pair of pants and shirt, made him feel somewhat more human than he had felt in a while. Refreshed, he headed for McGaa Street. It was not an impressive thoroughfare, though two buildings were substantial and rather fine looking, if not opulent. He found the one with a red door and opened it.

"Well, well, well, if it isn't Mr. Pike came to see me again," Clarissa said with a grin splitting her painted face.

"Howdy, Clarissa. I'm surprised you remember me. You must've had plenty of clients in the past few years."

"You're an intriguing man, Mr. Pike. With an unusual name. Same as the mountain not far from here."

"What're you doing in Denver, Clarissa?"

"I could ask you the same thing."

"I'm trail weary and needed time with some...people."

"The kind of people you'll find here, of course."

"Of course. But you never answered my question."

"Skeeter Creek started fading some months after the last time you stopped by my place there." She looked at him as if she were wondering about him. "There were a number of grisly killings, and people got spooked." Once again, the wondering look. "And the mines were playing out. People started leaving, slowly at first. After about a year I decided it was time to search for greener pastures. I had heard Denver was a booming place. So, here I am."

"I was somewhat surprised when Bart Blakely at the stables mentioned Clarissa's as the best place of its kind in Denver."

"You don't think my place is the best?" Clarissa asked in faux anger.

"I'm sure it is, but I never thought I'd find you up here and was thinkin' maybe there were two madams named Clarissa."

"If there's another, I'll gouge her eyes out," the madam said with a chuckle, which faded quickly. "You seem rather melancholy, Mr. Pike." When he said nothing, she smiled. "Well, one of my girls will put a sparkle back in your eye. I can guarantee that."

"I'm counting on it."

"Well, then, let me introduce you to Yvette. This young lady will boost your spirits. And something else!" She laughed.

Yvette did indeed lift his spirits. Enough so he could put aside his grieving for Little Raven for a little bit.

He visited Clarissa's twice more, once with Yvette and the other time with Savannah, who was in every way Yvette's equal in raising his spirits.

By then, though, he was getting low on cash and tiring of being around so many people. He didn't know why he didn't stop here to get some wanted posters, but he rode out of Denver and arrived in Boulder, where he stopped at the city marshal's office and picked up a handful of wanted posters. The next day, he rode out, heading west. Two days later he rode into Georgetown and stopped at the marshal's office there.

"I'm on the hunt for Ricketts Wiley. Heard he robbed the bank here."

"That he did, him and his men, three of 'em. Killed a teller and one of my deputies," Marshal Buster Argent said.

"Any idea where they ran off to when they left here?"

"I got up a posse and trailed 'em along South Clear

Creek but lost 'em before we got to the end of Guanella Pass. Men in the posse didn't want to go farther. Can't say I blame 'em."

"Mind if I try to run 'em down?"

"Hell no. I hope you catch the bastard and the ones who run with him."

"Obliged."

It took Pike almost a week, but he finally found Wiley and his three companions in a valley beyond the end of Guanella Pass, along Geneva Creek. They had set up a camp along a small stream that fed into the North Fork of the South Platte River. Pike almost rode out into the open before he realized the outlaws were there. He quickly pulled into the trees. Standing behind a spruce, he surveyed the landscape.

The men's camp was on the fringe of the forest, giving the outlaws quickly accessed cover. It would also allow Pike to sneak up close to the camp, except that there seemed to be no way to get there from where he was. Beyond the edge of the valley, the pine-covered hill rose quickly and there was no way he could circle around the tree line from here to behind the camp. At least from this side. It looked as if he could do so from the edge opposite him. but that could take some effort to accomplish. He'd have to go around another low, but steep, hill.

As if that wasn't enough trouble, it was dusk, and he did not want to go wandering around the hills and forests he did not know in the dark. He considered firing at them from where he was with the sniper rifle but discarded the idea. The outlaws were more than a hundred yards away, there was an unpredictable wind blowing, and daylight was fading fast. Besides, he didn't think he could get all four of them before at least a couple fled.

With a sigh, he mounted his horse and rode back the way he had come for a mile or so and stopped. He tended the animal and sat to a fine meal, he thought ruefully, of jerky and water. Bacon and coffee would be nice, but he could not risk a fire. He was far enough away from the outlaw's camp that it likely wouldn't be seen, but he could not be sure of that. So he settled in for his feast and soon turned to his bedroll.

Breakfast was more of the same. Then he was back in the saddle. A few miles later, again along the tree line, he surveyed the area and saw that the four men were still in their camp. Pike meandered through the trees, past rocky knobs of granite, large boulders, and thickets. Once he had to carefully ease the gelding's way around a hissing patch of rattlers, and twice he had to ride around deep gouges in the earth.

He finally made his way around the valley. With caution, he should be able to get into the trees right behind the camp and surprise the men. He began easing his way there, making every effort to not make noise, though he figured the men would not hear him with the talking they were doing, and their own horses snuffling and occasionally snorting.

He eventually reached a spot in the trees near the men's camp. He was not far from their horses and figured he could scatter the animals in a hurry if need be. He eased out a Colt and was ready to walk into the camp but stopped suddenly.

"Damn," he swore under his breath. There were only three men around the fire. That meant the fourth was...

A bullet tore bark off the tree near his head, and he flopped to the ground. "You idiot, Brodie. Ain't got the brains God gave a tree stump." He shook his head in anger at having not had the sense to make sure all the men were in the camp before plunging ahead. But he could not worry about that, and within a few seconds those thoughts scattered.

"Toby, what's goin' on?" Wiley shouted.

"Got me somebody treed. He was sneakin' up on the camp."

"Where?"

"About ten yard west of the horses. He heads this way, I got him. You boys spread out and he won't have nowhere to go."

Pike checked his options and realized he really had none. He was caught in a bad spot, and all he could do would be to fight it out.

He spun, yanked out his other Colt and charged toward the camp. As he had thought—or maybe just hoped—the move surprised Wiley and the two companions with him. Firing both pistols, Pike dropped all three. Dead or not, they were out of the fight for at least a short while.

A slug hit him high in the back, and he sank to a knee. Then he dropped and rolled as two more bullets tossed up dirt near where he had been. Lying on his stomach, Pike's eyes frantically searched for the gunman's location. Another slug kicked up dirt inches from his face.

"Give it up," the outlaw shouted.

"Like hell. I got your three pals, and I'll get you too, boy. Don't doubt that." Pike squirmed his way over to behind one of the bodies. It wasn't much protection, but it was better than being in the open as he had been. He glanced down to get whatever look he could at his wound. It was not as bad as he had thought, the bullet having just torn a chuck of muscle out of the top of his shoulder.

He caught a glimpse of a horse threading its way through the trees, heading the way Pike had come from. "Dammit all." He jumped up, ran to his horse, jumped on, and headed after the man. Moments later he was knocked out of his saddle by a large branch.

He landed with a painful thump. "Damn horse," he muttered as he picked himself up, glad that the tree limb had hit him in the chest instead of the head. He had a little trouble breathing but didn't think he had broken anything. He hurried to the tree line in time to see the outlaw disappear into the forest.

With an annoyed shake of the head, he went to the outlaws' fire. Some rabbit on a spit was close to burning, so Pike moved it. He lifted the coffeepot, pleased to find it half full or so.

He looked at the three bodies. "You boys can wait," he muttered. He sat and poured himself some coffee and sliced off a piece of rabbit, then ate it and another.

His horse wandered up nearby and stopped, cropping grass. "About time you got back here, you damned swaybacked flea bag." He went and hobbled the animals, then loaded the corpses on the men's horses, leaving the saddles where they were. Then he went back to the fire and ate some more.

As he sipped coffee, he looked at the sky. There was still plenty of daylight left, but it would be better to stay here in a camp already made. There was more rabbit to eat and more coffee to drink.

He unsaddled the horse and tended it, then polished off the one cooked rabbit. He sat, stewing in his anger at having let the last outlaw get away. He would have to rectify that as soon as he could. He would not rest until he did so.

CHAPTER FOUR

"Three of 'em?" Marshal Buster Argent said as he stopped in front of Pike on the street.

Anger flared in Pike.

Argent saw it and shook his head a little. "Didn't mean that as a complaint, Brodie. More like surprise that you could bring in three of the four by yourself."

The bounty hunter's anger did not ebb. "You don't think I'm capable?"

"Hell, Brodie. I would've been happy if you just brought in Wiley's corpse. Those boys've been mighty elusive."

"Did take me a while to find 'em," Pike admitted, temper easing.

"Looks like they got you," the lawman said, pointing to the side of Pike's neck.

His anger roared back, this time against himself. "I'm lucky I ain't dead," the bounty hunter snapped. "Wasn't paying enough attention to the number of men around the fire. There were only three. The fourth was behind me. I managed to get mostly out of the way, so the slug just skimmed me instead of plowin' a hole right through my back. I got the other three, but the one who shot me got away." He did not think it necessary to mention that he had been knocked off his horse by a tree branch.

"Well, I'd say it shows how good you are when you got three men while bein' wounded by another. Ain't too many men can have a shootout with three well-heeled outlaws by himself and win."

Pike just grunted acknowledgment, still displeased with himself. "What do I do with these three?"

"Take 'em to Sulkie's. Up a little ways and turn at Alliance Street." He looked around and suddenly yelled, "Chuckie, run down to Sulkie's and tell him he's got three new customers headin' his way."

"Right, Marshal," a boy of about twelve said and ran off.

"After you drop these three off and stable your animals, meet me at Greene's restaurant. I'll buy you a dinner."

"Sounds good." He turned and headed up the street.

* * *

"You going after the one who shot you, Brodie?"

"That's a damn fool question," Pike said around a mouthful of chicken and dumplings. He swallowed.

"Well, I've never said or done a damn fool thing in

my life, so I wanted to see how it would be." He grinned.

Pike looked at him as if he were insane, then burst out laughing. "So how do you feel?"

"Like a damn fool." He joined the laughter and grew serious. "I can't offer much help, Brodie, but I'll do what I can. Make sure you're supplied when you ride out, maybe, not much else I can do."

"Lookin' for a share of the reward money?"

Argent stiffened. "Now it's my turn to get resentful, Mr. Pike. I'm an honest lawman. An honest man. If Toby Calhoun rode into town and I managed to kill him, I'd be glad to take the reward money. But I'll be damned if I'll take money for something someone else has done. Now if you'll excuse me." He started to rise.

"Sit down, Buster." When the lawman did, Pike said, "I was pretty sure you were gonna say that, but I had to be certain."

"Such accusations don't sit well with me."

"Me neither. I didn't take kindly to some things you said when I rode into town this afternoon." He grinned. "Now we're even."

Argent grinned too. "Reckon we are."

"You could come with me," Pike suggested.

Argent thought that over for a minute or wo, then shook his head. "It's temptin', but I got a wife and three youngsters to think about. It was bad enough taking a posse out. My wife'd kill me if I decided to ride out with a bounty hunter."

"Women can get rather peevish over such things," the bounty hunter said. "Or so I've been told."

"You ever been married, Brodie?"

Pike considered that for a bit, then nodded. "Well, sort of. Didn't have it blessed by a preacher, but to us it was about the same."

"And she puts up with you bounty huntin'?" Argent asked, surprised.

"She did."

"You still with her?"

"She was killed."

"Did you…"

"There any more of that coffee left?" Pike asked, cutting him off.

The lawman lifted the pot, then called to the waiter for more. "Sorry, Brodie. Didn't mean to get so nosy."

"It's all right. Most folks would ask. But it's best left alone."

Argent nodded. He filled their cups and held his up in a salute. "To good women." He paused. "Or to those who are crazy enough to marry men like us."

"Amen to that."

* * *

Marshal Argent made sure Pike was well equipped when the bounty hunter rode out the next morning. He was going to protest but kept his mouth shut, figuring he would insult the lawman by saying anything.

He followed Guanella Pass to its end, then, relying on instinct more than anything else, cut west and southwest through a small pass and across a vast emptiness. It was then that he was thankful that Argent had made sure he was well supplied, though there were times when wood was hard to find, so a decent meal and some coffee were out of the question. But eventually he reached more favorable country and six days after he had left Georgetown, he reached South Park.

He wasn't sure which way to go then, but just pushed on. He was surprised when he saw a campfire in a large meadow. The tracks he had been following seemed to lead right to it. Still, he sat on his horse, thinking. He did not want to accost, let alone shoot, an innocent man. But there was no way to get close to the man to determine if it was the outlaw he was hunting for without being seen and thus risking taking a bullet himself.

He stayed in the fringe of trees more than a hundred yards away and waited. When darkness came, he moved forward on foot, towing the horse behind him. When he was about twenty-five yards from the fire, he swiftly slipped hobbles on the animal and left it, walking the rest of the way.

He stopped just outside the circle of firelight and waited a bit, until he could hear the man's soft breathing. He unlimbered a Colt and stepped up, looming over the sleeping man, fighting back the urge to just kill him and be done with it. But his better nature won out, mostly. He cocked his revolver, the soft sound making the man stir but not wake. With a grim grin, Pike fired, blasting off two fingers of Calhoun's outstretched right hand.

The outlaw howled and started to rise but fell back when his hand didn't work properly. He looked down and saw the missing digits, then looked up at Pike, who was smiling at him.

"What the hell'd you do that for?" Calhoun asked, pain and anger fighting for dominance in his voice.

"Payback for you shootin' me a week or so ago."

"Why you son of a…" He shut up when Pike knelt and tapped him on the forehead hard enough to get his attention but not enough to knock him out.

"I am not, as even an idiot like you might figure out, fond of bein' shot at, much less being shot. Now ease out your pistol, you'll likely have to use your left hand," he said, "and toss it gently toward me. If you have a belly gun, toss that too."

"I don't."

"I think you're lyin', and if I find one on you, you will regret it."

"In my right boot."

"Pull it easy and toss it."

When Calhoun had done so, Pike whacked him on the side of the head, disabling him enough that Pike could do what he needed to without resistance from the outlaw.

Pike got his horse and brought it to the camp and hobbled it again. Calhoun's animal was already so restricted, and the two stood there munching the grass. Against the outlaw's feeble protests, the bounty hunter shackled him hand and foot, then propped him up against his saddle. "Comfortable?"

"Go to hell."

"Maybe some other time." Pike squatted by the fire

and poured himself some coffee, then finished off what bacon there was in the frying pan.

"Enjoyin' yourself?" Calhoun asked in an irritated voice.

"Well, it's far from the best thing I ever ate, but it's better than nothin.'"

"What're you aimin' to do with me?"

"What do you think?"

"Kill me," the outlaw said matter-of-factly.

"If I was gonna do that, I would've done so already."

"Maybe, maybe not."

"What's that mean?"

"Means I still figure you're plannin' to kill me but you're gonna wait 'til we're closer to whatever town you plan on takin' me to. That way you don't have to drag around a ripenin' corpse. Get me within a day, or even a couple hours, of some town and put a bullet in me. Fresh body, no stink." He let loose a cackling laugh.

"Don't go giving me ideas, especially ones that make sense."

"Damn." Calhoun shook his head. "You got something to bandage my hand?" he asked. "It's hurtin' like the devil."

"Not unless you got a shirt or some socks in your saddlebags."

"Bandanna in there."

Pike got it and tossed it to Calhoun. "Wrap it yourself."

"Afraid I'll hit you even though I'm shackled?" he sneered.

"Just bein' cautious." Pike sat back down. When he saw that the outlaw had managed to roughly wrap his wounded hand, the bounty hunter said, "You best get some sleep. Be a long few days before I stick you in the hoosegow somewhere."

"You might be the one not to make it wherever we're goin'."

"I got a hell of a lot better chance than you." Pike spread out his bedroll and stretched out to lay on it. In minutes he was asleep.

It took almost a week to get to Georgetown, and the last two days he considered putting a bullet in the outlaw's heart. He was tired of cooking up breakfast and supper every day, tending to two horses, packing up and unloading supplies. It was irritating. As was Calhoun's frequent complaining. He resorted more than once to gagging the vociferous outlaw. But he kept on.

It was with considerable relief that he arrived in Georgetown with his prisoner still alive. Marshal Buster Argent was making his rounds when he spotted the new arrivals. He hurried up the street and fell into step alongside Pike's horse.

"I'm surprised he's still alive, Brodie," the lawman said with a grin.

"Not as much as I am," Pike said without one.

Argent looked up at him in surprise, then said, "No matter. I got a cell just waitin' for him."

"Hope it's not too comfortable."

"Don't matter," the outlaw said. "I won't be there long."

"If you think you can escape," Argent said, "you're

crazy. If you're thinkin' a lynch mob might invite you to a necktie party, well, that could very well mean you won't be there long."

Minutes later, they were at the marshal's office and minutes after that, Calhoun was ensconced in a cell.

"Was it hard?" Argent asked.

"Nah. Pain in my rump, but not difficult."

"Well, you just added another three hundred to the rest of the reward. Almost eleven hundred in total."

"Damn good sum."

"It is. You want to get paid in silver from the mines or someway else?"

"Silver's oaky, as long as it's in coins."

"Reckon we can do that. Come on over in the mornin' and I'll have it here."

* * *

"There it is," Argent said in the morning, pointing to a pouch on his desk. "All eleven hundred."

"I'll have to get a mule just to carry that," Pike said with a grin.

"Well, I could take some of it off your hands." Before Pike could glare at him, he laughed.

"Reckon you could." The bounty hunter picked up the bag, opened it and started counting.

"Don't trust me?" The marshal seemed a little upset.

"Yep, I do." He held out a handful of coins.

"What's that?" Argent asked, confused.

"A small payment for your help."

"I didn't..." The look on Pike's face told him to shut up and take the money. "What now, Brodie?" he asked as the bounty hunter closed the pouch.

"Hunt for more outlaws, I reckon."

CHAPTER FIVE

Brodie Pike was enjoying a meal in Parker's Chop House in Golden when a boy of about ten walked in, a stack of newspapers under one arm. In the other hand, he held a copy aloft as he announced, "Sheriff killed! Outlaw escapes!"

Pike called the boy over, gave him two pennies, took the copy of the newspaper, and stared at the front page. "Oh, sweet Lord Almighty," he muttered as he read the article near the top of the page.

Valiant Marshal Buster Argent of Georgetown was laid low by the outlaw Toby Calhoun during a bold escape from the town's jail.

Calhoun was being held on charges of murdering two citizens of the aforementioned town during a robbery of the National Bank some four weeks ago. He was brought to Georgetown to face justice by a bounty hunter who previously had dispatched the three other members of the gang led by Ricketts Wiley, of which Calhoun was a member.

Officials were awaiting the arrival of a territorial judge when the dishonorable fellow laid the marshal low in his run for freedom. A posse was unable to run down the miscreant, who is still on the loose.

Deputy Marshal Bob Ogden was also slain by the outlaw.

Mayor Josiah Hampton...

Leaving his meal unfinished, Pike tossed down a silver dollar, slapped on his hat and hurried out. Within an hour he was on his horse, his saddlebags filled with enough provisions for two days. Since it was afternoon when he left, he made it less than halfway, but he was on the trail again and riding hard.

While he traveled, he cursed himself repeatedly. Once again, he had caused harm when he meant to bring good. Like the time he had let Jed Axelrod live, and the outlaw had also escaped and went in a killing rampage until Pike had hunted him down a second time and put the scoundrel in the grave. This was the same. He wanted to see that Calhoun faced justice in front of the people he had offended, so Pike had brought him in alive, only to have the outlaw escape and kill a good lawman, a good man. Pike rode with teeth clenched in anger at himself for another disaster born of his desire to do good.

It was dusk when he reached Georgetown. Without a thought to proprieties, he hitched his horse to the rail in front of the mayor's house, walked up the few steps, and pounded on the door.

"Go away!" a voice came from inside.

"Open the door, Mayor, or I'll kick it in."

The official yanked open the door, anger stamped across his pudgy, ruddy face, a napkin tucked into his collar. "What in the name of all that's holy do you want?" he demanded. Then he recognized Pike. "You!" he said, surprised. "Come in, come in."

The mayor led Pike to the dining room, where a servant girl was just clearing away the remains of supper. "Irma, Agnes, Hiram," he said to his wife, daughter, and son, "please go into the sitting room. Rosie, some coffee for Mr. Pike." To the latter, he said, "Sit, please."

Moments later, Rosie placed a cup of coffee in front of the bounty hunter and left as Hampton waved her away. "So, I assume you heard about Buster."

"Yep. It's why I'm here."

"Marshal Argent was a good man."

"Yes, sir, he was. And I aim to see that he gets justice, no matter how delayed it might be. I should've planted him in the boneyard in the first place."

"You did right by bringing him in alive, Mr. Pike, is it?"

The bounty hunter nodded.

"It was important that he face his peers...well, the citizens of Georgetown who he so outraged."

"That was my thought. I now think that thinkin' was misplaced."

"No matter now. It's over and done, and the only thing to be done is to see that Calhoun pays the full price for his deviltry."

"I aim to see that he does." Pike paused for a sip of coffee. "Did Calhoun have any help?"

"We don't think so. Just lack of attention by Deputy Ogden. Best we can tell, Calhoun had been behaving himself, which made Ogden lax, thinking Calhoun was resigned to his fate. When he went to take Calhoun his supper, he foolishly stepped inside the open door instead of just opening it a bit and sliding the tray inside. Calhoun took advantage. Seems he clouted Ogden in the head, grabbed the deputy's gun, shot him, charged out of the back and shot Buster in the side of the head as the marshal was getting up to investigate. Calhoun grabbed Buster's revolver, ran outside, stole the nearest horse, and lit out. By the time anyone realized what had happened, he was long gone."

"Posse chase him?"

"Yes," Hampton said with a sigh of resignation. "But they took mighty long to get organized with no lawmen around to organize things."

"Georgetown had only one deputy?" Pike was surprised.

"Yes. We had three, but two had quit, heading out to seek their fortune in the gold fields. We hadn't gotten around to replacing them yet."

"Which way was he headed?"

"West. Of course, he might've switched back just outside of town. If he kept west, I figure he'd turn southwest for Breckenridge, the only town out that way as far as I know, though others might've sprung up."

"All right. Thanks, Mayor." Pike finished his coffee and started to rise.

"Wait, Mr. Pike." When the bounty hunter had retaken his seat and looked at Hampton in question, the mayor said, "You look like you've ridden hard. Don't know where you came in from, but wherever it was, I don't think you left this morning. It's almost dark. Take the night to get some rest. In the morning we can get you some supplies and you can head out refreshed."

"I need to get on the trail."

"It's been a week. One more night won't make a difference."

It went against Pike's grain, but he knew Hampton was right. He reluctantly nodded.

"You hungry?"

Pike realized he was and nodded.

"Rosie," Hampton called. When the girl appeared, the mayor said, "bring a plate of roast and everything else for Mr. Pike. And more coffee."

"Yes, sir." She was back in little more than a minute with a plate spilling over with roast beef, potatoes, and green beans. She went back to the kitchen and returned with a coffeepot. She refilled his cup, then placed the pot on the table. She curtsied and left.

Pike hungrily dug in. When the bounty hunter had finished, Hampton asked, "A snort or two?"

"Just one."

Hampton poured Pike a half cup of whiskey, then called to his son. When the twelve-year-old popped in, he looked eager as he thought he would be included in the men's discussion. He was disappointed when his father said, "Take Mr. Pike's horse to the livery, then…"

"No," Pike said. At Hampton's surprised look, the bounty hunter said, "My gear and such is valuable to me, and I try not to let anyone touch it. I'll stable the horse myself. I'd appreciate it, though, if you could arrange a hotel."

"As you wish. Hiram, go see Mr. Blake at George's Inn and get Mr. Pike a room. Tell Mr. Blake that the city will pay for it and that it should be the best room available. Then get Mr. Pike at the stables and bring him to the hotel. Understood?"

"Yes, Pa." The boy hurried out.

Pike left moments later and rode to the livery stable. He took his saddlebags, Henry rifle, and the sniper rifle in its special scabbard. Hiram was waiting outside.

"Wow, that's some fancy rifle you got there, Mr. Pike," the boy gushed, pointing at the sniper rifle.

"That it is." He smiled. "And it's not for young boys."

Hiram pouted a minute, then cheered up as he led the bounty hunter to the hotel.

* * *

Pike considered protesting when he saw the mule laden with supplies waiting for him when he went into the stable to saddle his horse. Then he decided against it. The people of Georgetown meant well, and it was a sign of the respect they had for the late

Marshal Buster Argent. So he took the rope to the mule in hand, nodded his thanks for those townsfolk who had gathered to send him off, and rode on out.

With no way to track Calhoun, Pike rode for Breckenridge following the trail Mayor Hampton had scratched out on a piece of paper. The journey went from gulch to hill to gully, past steep cliffs and jumbles of gigantic boulders. He often traveled close to Clear Creek, until he cut south along Blue River. With all the obstacles, it took Pike almost three full days to make it, and he arrived in Breckenridge in midafternoon. The town was far smaller and less populated than he had expected.

The bounty hunter's first stop was at the livery stable, where he left the horse to the owner's care, and the mule's supplies to his assistant. He got a room in the town's only hotel, an unprepossessing place, where he left his gear. Then he set about tracking down the marshal, whom he found chatting with the owner of the town's sole mercantile store. He let the lawman ignore him for a couple of minutes, then cleared his throat and said, slightly less than politely, "A word with you, Marshal?"

"When I'm done talkin' to Edgar here," the marshal said dismissively.

"If I was to shoot Edgar would that get me your undivided attention?"

The lawman's head whipped around and a hand reached toward the butt of his holstered old Colt worn haphazardly almost on one hip. He stopped when Pike shook his head. "What's this about?" he asked in a voice that was not all that steady.

"Might be best to talk outside, or in your office."

"All right, my office, then."

"What's your name, by the way?"

"Elwood Bagby." He led the way out.

As they walked toward the office, Pike appraised the lawman and was not impressed. Bagby was several inches shorter than Pike, and rather stout. He was comfortably into middle age, with the creases and lines in his face that came with it. He was poorly dressed, had longish hair spilling out of a mouse-colored, sweat-stained hat, and had a long, scraggly mustache.

Bagby unlocked his office door and stepped inside, followed by Pike. "So, what is it you wanted to talk to me about?" the marshal asked. His nervousness was evident in his voice.

"Toby Calhoun."

The blood drained from the lawman's face. "What about him?"

"You seen or heard anything about him lately?"

"Well, I..."

"Marshal Bagby," Pike said in even, measured tones that were laced with iron, "I am in a foul humor, and I am in no mood to spend time trying to dig information out of you. The son of a bitch killed a good man in Georgetown, and..."

"Marshal Argent?"

"Yep. And I feel at least some responsibility for that. To make amends for that as much as is possible, I intend to hunt the bastard down and make him pay full price for what he did. Mayor Hampton in Georgetown said Calhoun seemed to be headed this way when he fled after gunnin' down Marshal Argent and his deputy. So this is the best place to start. If you know something, I would be mighty obliged if you were to tell me."

"But what if you're a friend of…"

"I ain't. I'm the fella who brought him in to Georgetown in the first place. I should've killed him before I did, but I didn't. So I'm responsible for Marshal's Argent's death. Now, have you seen Calhoun or heard of him?"

"He was here more than a week ago. Spent two, no, three, days here. Roughed up a few citizens and robbed a couple of miners of whatever gold they had, which wasn't much."

"And you didn't do anything about it?"

Bagby squirmed. "I ain't tough enough to go against a man like that," he said, the crimson of shame splashing across his face.

"Reckon you're right about that." Pike eased up a bit. "Ain't many men are. Which way was he headed?"

"Mostly east far as I know. Ain't much out there and the trail turns mostly south."

"Maybe. Anything distinctive I can hope to pick up and track 'em with?"

"Not really. Just a horse and a mule. I figured there ain't many other folks out there, so if you find those tracks it'll likely be him."

"You've been a big help," Pike said, doing little to disguise the sarcasm in his voice.

CHAPTER SIX

Brodie Pike stopped his gelding and looked out over the small expanse of the meadow, shaking his head in disbelief. There was Toby Calhoun sitting at a fire in almost the exact same spot he and his cohorts had been when Pike last confronted them. He dismounted and started to pull his sniper rifle from the special scabbard, then stopped with it halfway out. "No," he muttered. "That won't do."

He loosened the saddle's cinch to allow the horse to breathe and stood where he was for a while, watching and making sure Calhoun was alone. As dusk faded into night, Pike saw Calhoun bed down near the fire. The bounty hunter tightened the cinch, mounted, and rode through the trees around toward the outlaw's camp. He finally stopped just a few yards into the trees in front of the camp, dismounted, and tied the sorrel gelding to a bush.

The feeling of déjà vu swarmed over him as he strode out, then stopped, looming over the outlaw.

The strangeness of the situation almost fogged his mind, but he shook it off. But to continue with the oddness, he cocked the Colt, which made Calhoun stir and shift a little. Pike shot off two fingers of the outlaw's left hand.

Calhoun screeched and sat up, hand reaching for his Colt. Missing the fingers from his earlier capture made it difficult, and he quickly learned that he could not use his left hand either.

"I should've done both hands the last time," the bounty hunter growled. "If I had, Marshal Argent and Deputy Ogden would still be alive."

"I would've managed," Calhoun hissed, teeth clenched against the pain. "That deputy was as dumb as a horseshoe. Or maybe just too trustin'." He gave off with a phlegmy laugh.

"Good men can sometimes be too trustin'. It's what makes 'em good men."

"Also makes 'em dead when they come across a man like me."

"Sadly, that's true. Trouble is, I ain't that trustin'."

"Sure you are. You weren't, you would've killed me last time and saved me the trouble of having to blast those two damned lawmen."

Pike gritted his teeth at the truthfulness of those words.

"And you're bein' too trustin' by not puttin' me in my grave now. You should've just put a slug in my head while I was sleepin'."

"Should have. But, well, you had a good idea last time."

"Oh, what's that?" Calhoun seemed perplexed.

"You suggested I shoot you dead just before we got to Georgetown so I wouldn't have to drag along a ripenin' corpse for miles. I do believe that'd suit me just fine this time."

"It's a long way to Georgetown."

"I got you there last time. In one piece, mostly. I'll do it again, though maybe not in one piece."

"Don't be so sure you'll make it."

Pike grinned nastily. "Oh, you can count on me gettin' there alive. Can't say the same for you. Now lay down on your belly with your hands behind your back."

"Hell if I will." His grin was insolent.

The bounty hunter kicked the outlaw under the jaw, knocking him back, dazed. Pike slid his revolver away, grabbed a rope and tied Calhoun up, the rope going from around his neck the hands, then feet, with no break. "Comfy?" Pike asked, his voice harsh.

Still dazed, Calhoun nonetheless managed to curse in a steady stream, until Pike sliced off the outlaw's bandanna and shoved it in his mouth. Satisfied, he knelt at the fire and poured some coffee. Then he rummaged around and found some bacon in Calhoun's saddlebags. He cooked some and ate hungrily though without enthusiasm.

He tended to the gelding after eating, then turned in. He was asleep quickly, but he slept lightly. In the morning, he ate again, then saddled the horses. He left the frying pan and coffeepot where they were, though he took what bacon and coffee Calhoun had left and put them in his own saddlebags. When he went to grab Calhoun, the outlaw's eyes bugged out a little, and he tried to speak. Pike pulled the gag out of his mouth.

"I got to go to the bushes, take care of business."

"No, you don't." Pike jammed the gag back into Calhoun's mouth. He loosened the rope tying the outlaw a little so he could toss the man over the saddle of his horse, belly down, then tied him that way. Calhoun tried screaming his rage but little more than muffled protests came out.

Two days later, after Pike had eaten that morning, he propped Calhoun in a sitting position against his saddle and pulled the gag from the outlaw's mouth. "Damn, if you don't stink," the bounty hunter remarked, almost cheerfully.

"I'll kill you for this," Calhoun managed to gargle, mouth dry from lack of water and disuse.

"Oh, I don't think you will. Now, if you're hungry, I'll feed you a bit. You sass me, I'll gag you again and let you starve." He held out a piece of bacon, and Calhoun eagerly gulped it down, then another.

"Coffee," Calhoun said.

Pike filled a tin cup and poured some into the outlaw's mouth. Calhoun spit it out, splattering Pike's face and shirt. His grin froze on his face when he saw the look in Pike's eyes.

The bounty hunter gently placed the cup on the ground, then slammed a fist into Calhoun's face, shattering his nose. He shoved the gag back in the outlaw's mouth. Then he stood and stomped his boot heel down on Calhoun's left kneecap. It shattered with a loud snap.

The outlaw's eyes seemed as if they were about to

pop out of his head, and the veins on his neck stood out as he tried to scream out the pain around the bandanna in his mouth. Not much sound came out, and for a few moments, Pike thought the outlaw might swallow the gag. But Calhoun passed out.

Pike saddled both horses, threw Calhoun's inert, foul-smelling body over the outlaw's animal, and pulled out. Over the next three days, he neither fed Calhoun nor allowed him to drink. He considered leaving him tied across the saddle all the time but decided that would be unfair to the horse.

Finally, he was within sight of Georgetown. He dismounted and grabbed Calhoun's hair, lifting his head up. "We're about at our destination, Mr. Calhoun, and you will make a grand entrance for the good folks of Georgetown. He pulled the outlaw down from the horse and tied another rope around Calhoun's ankles. The other end was dallied around the saddle horn on the man's horse.

As he mounted his gelding, rage, self-disgust, and exhaustion swept over him. It was, he decided, an appropriate mix of feelings considering the situation and what had brought him to this point. He took the reins to Calhoun's horse, looked back, and said, "Here we go, Mr. Calhoun. Enjoy the ride." He kicked his horse into motion.

They raced into town, Calhoun's body bouncing along in the horse's wake, scraping through the dirt, rolling over and over as the land tore at his skin and eventually bones.

At the far end of town, Pike pulled the two horses around and started back up Rose Street, which was suddenly lined with townsfolk, watching intently, the women and children in horror.

The bounty hunter pulled to a stop in front of Sulkie's. The undertaker cautiously came out of his establishment and looked at what was left of Toby Calhoun. "That who I think it is?" he asked.

"If you're thinkin' it's Marshal Argent's killer, yep."

Angus Sulkie nodded. "In my professional opinion this man is in need of my services." He paused. "I'm not sure, however, that I am willing to provide them."

"Understandable. But I'm sure you can figure something out."

"I reckon I can."

Sulkie turned as Mayor Josiah Hampton rushed up. The official looked up at Pike, who was still mounted. "Calhoun?"

"One and the same," Pike said flatly. "Might not be recognizable, though. Seems he had a disfigurin' accident."

"I can see that." Hampton looked at Sulkie. "Can you do anything?"

"Doubt it, but even if I could, I wouldn't, not after what this man has done."

"Not even dispose of him?"

Sulkie thought that over. "I suppose I can have Andy hack him apart and toss the pieces down that old two-holer behind the building where the assay office used to be."

"Sounds appropriate. What'll it cost for it?"

"Two dollars ought to be enough."

"I'll pay it," Hampton said.

"No," Pike interjected. "I'll pay it. I feel I owe it to Marshal Argent and Deputy Ogden."

Both Hampton and Sulkie nodded. The latter called for a disheveled middle-aged man who had been peeking around the corner of the mortuary. "You heard?" Sulkie asked when the man sidled up.

"Yes, sir," he mumbled.

"Then get to it. Do your work where you'll deposit the body parts." He looked at Pike. "Can he take Calhoun's horse over there with the body?"

"Yep. Just bring the animal to the livery when he's done." He handed the reins to Andy. Before the man could lead the animal away, Pike reached into a pocket and pulled out four silver dollars. "That should be more than enough."

Sulkie looked at him as if he were going to protest, but then nodded. "Go on, Andy."

"Head on over to the stable yourself, Mr. Pike," Hampton said. "I'll arrange a room for you at George's Inn. I can also make sure the tonsorial parlor is waiting for you, if you wish." It was a question.

"That would be good, Mayor. I might stop off at Kline's for a new outfit. This one's a mite gamey."

Hampton smiled. "I didn't want to say anything, but it is true. I'll stop by Kline's too and tell him to send me the bill for whatever you need."

"That's not necessary. I can pay my own way."

"Yes, it is necessary. You've done a great service to the people of Georgetown, and we owe you much for that."

Pike decided not to argue. "It might sound mercenary, but I expect there's another reward on Calhoun."

"There is. Five hundred, put up by the National Bank of Georgetown. I'll speak with Mr. Gadsden, the banker, and have him arrange payment to you tomorrow, if that's acceptable."

"It is."

* * *

Despite a hot soak in a tub, a shave, and haircut, Pike was not much more peaceful than he had been when he rode into Georgetown. He was still plagued by the thought that he had brought about the two lawmens' deaths.

A decent meal, an hour in a decent brothel, and two beers helped a little, and he was able to sleep fairly well.

Mayor Josiah Hampton and banker Ellsworth Gadsden were waiting for him at the bank in the morning. The latter seemed just a trifle reluctant to hand over the money, until Hampton cast a gimlet eye on him.

Gadsden handed Pike the money, and said, "You've done the citizens of Georgetown a great service."

Pike simply nodded and took the sack of gold and silver coins. Then he walked outside with Hampton. "Should I count it?" he asked.

"No. Ellsworth might be stingy but when he pays what's due, he pays in full."

Pike nodded again.

"So what'll you do now. Brodie?"

The bounty hunter stood in thought for a few

moments, then asked, instead of answering the question, "Buster said he had a wife and kids. Did Ogden?"

"Yes. Why?"

"I'd like to meet them. Pay my respects."

"I'm not sure that's..." Hampton stopped, then nodded. "Let's go."

CHAPTER SEVEN

Miriam Argent was a tall woman grown a little stout after the birth of three children, though still attractive and normally, Pike thought, full of life. Now her face was clouded with mourning, her blue eyes dull with the pain of loss.

"This is Mr. Pike," Mayor Hampton said. "He's the one who...extracted justice for Buster's..."

"I hope I'm not intruding, ma'am," Pike interjected hastily. "I wanted to extend my condolences for your loss. I didn't know Marshal Argent long, but I knew him to be an honest lawman and a good man."

"Thank you." She paused. "I hate to be rude, Mr. Pike, is it? But I must see to the children." She started to close the door.

Pike stopped it. "I understand, ma'am. But before I go, please take this with my condolences." He held out a small pouch that jingled when the woman took it.

"What is this?" she asked surprised.

"Just a bit to tide you over for a spell is all."

Miriam looked into the pouch and tears formed in her eyes. "Thank you, Mr. Pike. It would come in handy, but I can't take this." She held it out.

"Yes, you can, ma'am."

"But it's your...I'm sure it's the reward for catching that...that..."

"Yes, that man, though I'd use a much harsher term in the company of just men. Like I said, I knew Buster to be a good man, and did a hard job as best he could to raise a fine family. And as such, he earned this as much as I did. It'll tide you over 'til you can settle his affairs and such."

"But I..."

"Good day, ma'am. Again, my sympathies." Pike turned and, with Hampton in his wake, stepped off the tidy house's porch.

* * *

The scene was repeated at the home of Lilith Ogden, a shorter, plumper, and poorer woman than Miriam Argent but no less as dignified, even in her suffering, as the marshal's wife. She, too, was hesitant to take the money until Pike insisted. He tipped his hat when she did and left with Hampton.

As the two men walked down the street, Hampton said, "You're a better, more decent man than your profession usually produces."

Pike shrugged, embarrassed by the praise.

"So what'll you do now?"

"Don't know, exactly. Find some more outlaws to chase after, I reckon. It's what I do."

"Have you been doing it long?"

"Too long, but it's all I know, and I'm good at it." *When I'm not causin' more harm than good*, he thought.

"Well, I hope you'll enjoy the hospitality of our fine town, Brodie. For a few days, at least."

"I likely will." Pike had no such intention, really. He figured another day would be enough.

"And I insist you come to supper at my house this evening."

"I ain't so sure your wife and children will be welcomin' to such a man as myself."

"I think they'll be fascinated by dining with a courageous and determined man like you. We'll see you at six." Hampton turned and headed for his office, not waiting to hear if Pike accepted or protested.

* * *

Instead of heading north toward Middle Boulder, where he could start tracking Ben Sykes and his gang, Pike found himself heading south. He knew where he was going but he was loath to admit it to himself. A week later, he stopped at a cave in a hill above a pleasant little valley. He unsaddled the horse and unloaded the mule and tended both.

Finally, he walked slowly toward the stone that marked where Little Raven lay. "I miss you, woman," he said softly, his words carried off by the light breeze. "You were a fine woman and took good care of me. You would've been a great mother to our child too."

He clenched his teeth against the sadness that

threatened to overwhelm him and the tears he would not let come. "Your family knows," he continued. "I told Blind Bull and Crazy Hawk and all the others. They mourn for you properly, something I don't know how to do in your people's way. But I have been grievin', Raven, don't you doubt that. I just had to do it in my own way, and that meant going away for a spell to do what I do—chasin' outlaws. It gives me purpose, even if it brings trouble to innocent people too often."

He managed to conjure up a smile. "But before I did, after I placed you and our unborn child here, I went after the bastards who did this. Your own people, as I figure you knew.

* * *

Burying Little Raven was almost as difficult and heartrending as ending the suffering—and life—of young Winter Sky, the eleven-year-old Ute who had been so monstrously abused by a gang of whites. It had torn out his heart to have to do that to that little girl, and he was sure he would never forget the horror and pain of that. Burying his wife and unborn child was the second hardest thing he had ever had to do. But, as he had with the evil men who had so dreadfully abused Winter Sky, he was determined to find and kill the men who had done this.

First, even before he lay his wife to rest, he had to cauterize the wound where the arrow had pierced the side of his stomach, just below the bottom rib. He was losing a fair amount of blood after yanking the shaft free, and he almost passed out. But he gritted his teeth and set his knife in the fire. When it was glowing red, he took it, sucked in a deep breath against the pain he knew was coming, and slapped the steel on the wound. The skin hissed and the smell of burning flesh arose. He moaned. He pulled the knife free after a couple of seconds, and fell to the side, gasping with the pain and shock.

He lay there for some time—he didn't know how long—before he was able to rise. He ate some of the elk meat that had been kept warm near the fire. It gave him a little strength. At last Pike stood. Keeping his mind blank, he found a suitable spot for a grave a few yards from the cave and began digging. Then, with heavy heart, he wrapped Little Raven in one of their buffalo sleeping robes and lowered her small body into the hole.

"Damn," he muttered, repeating the curse with every shovelful of dirt he tossed into the grave. Done, Pike tramped the mound of dirt down, then piled rocks over it. Lastly, he found an odd-shaped boulder and struggled to carry and roll it until it rested at the head of the grave.

"It ain't much, Raven," he said in a voice shaky from the pain of loss and the pain of his wound. "But it's the best I can do. Don't matter how I bury you, though, you'll soon be in heaven, either yours or mine or both." Through the tears that had slipped out, he managed a grin. "And I'll say farewell to you for all time now, woman, for it'll be the last time I see you since there ain't no way I'll be following you to such a place. I reckon the devil's preparin' accommodations for me."

Dark was coming on fast, so Pike had to resist the urge to ride out now on the trail of the Utes who had done this. He settled for more food, then curled up on their other robe and was asleep almost instantly.

In the morning Pike finished the last of the elk as well as the last of the coffee in the pot. He packed a few supplies in a couple of buckskin sacks and filled two canteens from the nearby stream. He hung the sacks over the back of Little Raven's pinto, one hanging to each side, then saddled his own horse. He was tempted to just leave what had been their home the way it was but decided that it might tempt anyone who came along to dig up the grave, even though it was amid the trees some yards off, looking for anything worth money. He scatted the fire, tossed whatever gear that was left in the stream, and ran brush around the entire area. Finally, he shrugged. Pike mounted the sorrel and towing the gelding he rode out.

Pike wasn't the best tracker around but following the trail of the Utes was easy enough—unshod horses and drops of blood made it clear. Pike also decided they were in no hurry, which surprised him. If they thought they were safe, he wondered why they didn't come to take his and Little Raven's scalps? He decided that they wanted to get away with their wounded and that the scalps and anything else in the camp was not worth risking a dying but still-dangerous enemy.

By midafternoon of the following day, he sensed that he was getting close. He slowed, not wanting to run into them on the trail. Shortly before dusk, he smelled smoke, then thought he heard voices. He dismounted and tied both horses to a hackberry bush. He checked both Colts, then began easing his way through the trees. He stopped behind a large chokecherry bush and surveyed the Ute camp amid a small open spot dotted with well-spaced trees.

Pike counted the horses, then the men. There were half a dozen of each. Two of the men were lying on blankets. The bounty hunter figured they were the two he had wounded. The other warriors were squatting around a fire over which some meat, hanging from green sticks, was roasting.

Pike could see no reason to wait. He drew both revolvers and stepped out from behind the large bush. The Utes were unaware of his presence until two of them saw two others' heads explode from .44-caliber bullets. The two untouched ones leaped up, one heading toward Pike, the other headed for the trees.

Pike shot the one rushing him twice in the chest, then fired several shots at the fleeing man. The first fell dead at his feet, the other was hit three times, and fell. He tried to crawl away. The bounty hunter walked toward that one, reloading his pistols on the way.

Looming over the warrior, he asked, "Why'd you kill one of your own people?"

"She was with you, a white man."

"Pretty poor reason." He cocked a Colt. "She sends her regards from the afterworld, a place you likely ain't going." He shot the man in the throat.

He walked to where the two wounded Utes were

trying to get at their knives, their bows being nowhere close to hand. "Those won't do you no good, boys," Pike said. He shot each man in the stomach, then went to the fire and began eating some of the deer meat. He watched the two men writhe in pain. By the time Pike finished eating, they were dead.

CHAPTER EIGHT

"I couldn't come back to your grave then, Raven," Pike said, standing over his wife's grave. "That's why I'm here now. It was time. Those boys paid the price for their deviltry." He grinned harshly. "I even managed to get some good money when I drove all their horses to Colorado Springs and sold 'em. Folks there seemed mighty pleased that I rubbed out a bunch of renegade Utes."

He rose and said another prayer. "Rest well, Raven, and savor your life in the Spirit World."

Without another word, he stalked to his horse, mounted up and rode away. "Time to get back to work," he muttered. "Ben Sykes, your days of freedom are growing short."

* * *

Almost a week later he rode into Golden. The weather on the ride had been poor, the hunting even worse, so he decided it was time to take a breather. He stabled his horse, visited a tonsorial parlor, had a fine meal, got a room, and a good night's sleep. The next evening found him at Little Martha's.

In the morning, Pike was feeling pretty well. A night in a good sporting house with a beautiful buxom belle who called herself Sweet Charlotte put a spring in his step. A fine breakfast added to his enjoyment of the crisp, clean air of the town. He headed back to his hotel. As he went to insert the key in the lock, he saw that the door was slightly ajar.

Easing out a pistol, he inched the door open and waited a few moments, then kicked it all the way open. He poked his head around the jamb and glanced around. The only place a man could hide was under the bed, and that would take some doing.

He holstered his pistol and stepped inside and stopped. His saddlebags were lying on the floor—the flaps open. They were flat, meaning that everything that had been in them had been removed. Some of the items—a coffeepot, frying pan, utensils, an extra shirt—were scattered about the room. He was certain the several hundred dollars he had kept there was gone. The worst, though, was that his highly prized sniper rifle, and the special scabbard it rested in, were gone. As was his Henry rifle. He stood for some moments, trying to let the rage settle down some. He finally turned and headed to the front desk.

"Can I help you?" the deskman asked.

Pike stared for a moment, noting the smirk the man was trying to hide. He breathed deep, then asked,

"You seen anyone around here who doesn't belong here?"

"Well, surely not. Is something wrong?" The sneer had widened.

"I don't think you're being exactly truthful, Mr. Bennett."

"That so?"

"It is." Pike grabbed him by the shirt, yanked him forward a bit, then slammed a fist into Bennett's face, breaking his nose. Blood spurted out, barely mussing Pike's shirt. "Do I need to ask again? If so, I will add more emphasis than I just did."

"Not necessary," the man mumbled. "Fella named Monte Griffin."

"You help him?"

"Yes."

"Why?"

"Gave me ten dollars for the key."

"Where is he?"

"Don't know exactly." He shivered as Pike cocked his fist again. "He was heading to Denver."

"When did he leave?"

"Not long after you left here. He was watching you. When you headed to Little Martha's he figured you'd be a while, so he come in here."

"Damn. What's he ridin'?"

"Dun gelding."

"All right, you're going with me to my room and pack what he left into my saddlebags. Then you'll give me that ten dollars he gave you, plus another twenty for the annoyance you brought. If you think of settin' the marshal on me, I will come back here and shoot you dead. Is that understood?"

Bennett nodded nervously.

Twenty minutes later he was riding out of Golden. Late that afternoon, he rode into Denver. He left his horse, along with saddle and saddlebags, at the livery stable and walked down the street. He had seen Thompson's hardware and thought that would be a good place to start.

Pike saw the rifle propped in a prominent place on the wall behind the counter as soon as he walked in. He impatiently waited while a customer got his nails and hinges and left. Pike stepped up.

"What can I do for you, Mister?" the store owner asked.

Pike pointed. "Nice rifle and scabbard."

"Sure is. Never really saw one like it."

"It's mine."

"But…"

"And I want it back."

"Now wait a minute, Mister, I paid good money for that rifle and scabbard. You think I'm just gonna give it to the first fella walks in and claims it's his?"

"Well, yes, when the fella who comes in is the owner."

"I can't know that."

"My name's Brodie Pike. If you look on the underside of the stock where it comes off the lock, you'll see 'B. Pike'."

Thompson pulled out the rifle, doing so with the reverence such a fine weapon deserved, Pike noted, and checked. His face suddenly got downtrodden. He nodded. "Well, I got no way to be sure you're Pike, but the name is where you said it'd be." He slid the Sharps back into the special scabbard. With a shake of the head, he handed it gently to Pike.

The bounty hunter nodded. "Obliged."

"Yeah," Thompson said sadly. "There's two hundred fifty bucks gone out of my pocket."

"I'll also take my old Henry back." He pointed to the long arm resting carelessly on a back shelf.

Thompson handed it to him. "Not much of a loss on that one," he said with a sigh.

"It was a loss to me, Pike said. "What'd the fella who sold you these look like?"

"A little shorter than you, a little stouter. Nothing special about his look, though his hat was a mess. A mouse-gray Stetson that looked as if it had been run over by a herd of buffalo."

"Shirt? Pants?"

"Nothing out of the ordinary. Faded blue work shirt, striped trousers you can find on half the men in Denver."

"He say where he was going?"

"Hinted that he'd be at Lulu's brothel but he's such a slob I doubt Lulu would let him in the door even if he had the money, which he does now. So probably hit one of the cribs behind the Gold Leaf or Silver Bell. But that would've been a while ago."

"Thanks." Pike walked out. On the boardwalk he wondered what he should do. Considering what had happened in Golden, he was reluctant to leave the weapons in a hotel room. On the other hand, he could not wander around Denver carrying them. And he wanted to find Griffin. He finally decided it would have to be a hotel room. He got one and stashed the two rifles under the bed, then headed out.

He got lucky. He spotted a man with a trampled hat in the Gold Leaf. As Pike neared the man, Griffin turned partially, and the bounty hunter got a glimpse of his face. "Well, I'll be..." He marched up to the man. "Good evenin', Mr. Crump."

The man started, then settled down. "You got the wrong fella. My name's Griffin. Monte Griffin."

"Lying to a man who holds your life in his hands is mighty foolish, Clarence. Now, me and you are gonna walk outside and have us a little discussion. If you give me a hard time about it, you will regret it. Now, let's go."

"And if I don't want to?" He smirked, thinking he had the upper hand in a saloon full of men. "Are you gonna shoot me?"

"I could do that. But that'd be noisy, even in a place like this. But a knife to your innards wouldn't make much noise."

"You wouldn't do that," Crump said, suddenly afraid.

"Yes, I would. Now, let's go." Outside, he demanded, "Where's my money, Clarence?"

"At my room in the boarding house."

"Then by all means, let us go retrieve it." Pike gave Crump a shove. More shoves were necessary as Crump tried walking slower and slower, as if he were marching to his doom.

They finally made it, and Pike watched carefully, a hand on a pistol, as Crump rummaged around under the bed. He finally came up with a sack that jingled. "It's all there," he said.

"It better be. Where's the money Thompson gave you for the rifles?"

"Spent some of it."

"Then give me the rest."

"I won't have anything left," Crump whined.

"I am filled with sympathy. Hand it over." To emphasize his point, Pike punched Crump in the face.

The outlaw pulled another, smaller sack from under the bed, stood shakily, and handed it to Pike.

"Good. Now empty your pockets."

"But..."

The bounty hunter punched him again, and Crump handed over all the money—coins and paper—he had. "See, that wasn't so hard, was it, Clarence?" He suddenly drove a fist into the outlaw's stomach. Crump doubled over and fell to his knees, desperately trying to breathe.

Pike set the two sacks on the bed, then said, very distinctly, each word accompanied by a punch, "I. Don't. Like. When. People. Steal. My. Property." He stopped and picked up the sacks of money and left.

CHAPTER NINE

Pike was a few miles north of Golden, heading toward Middle Boulder, when he stopped. He sat a few minutes, thinking. Then he decided. He turned south, skirting the town. Five days later he sat on the slight bluff looking at Charlie McAllister's place. It looked more finished, more of a comfortable home. Pike was pleased to see it. He rode on down. A man came out of the house, holding a rifle. The bounty hunter was surprised that it wasn't McAllister. Then he recognized Connor Felder.

"Well, I'll be," Felder said when Pike rode up. "Never thought I'd see you again. Welcome, Brodie."

"Howdy, Con. Your family move in with Charlie here?"

"Nope. Charlie's moved over to Hungerford's old place.

"When did that happen?"

"About six months after you left." He was a little surprised at the look of annoyance that had slid onto

Pike's face, but he said nothing about it. "Why don't you come inside. It's a little early yet, but we can have coffee. Becca will have supper on soon."

"I reckon Becca would rather old Beelzebub came to supper before me, Con," Pike said with a chuckle. He had noticed a slight movement inside the house through the partially open door and figured it was Felder's wife.

"Well, now that you mention it..." Felder laughed.

"Take care, Con. Give my regards to all the others."

"I will, but some'll not be happy to have missed you, especially the young men, Arch and Will and Vin."

"Probably give 'em nightmares if they saw me." He tipped his hat, then shouted, "You can relax, Becca. I'm leavin'." He laughed again when the door slammed. He rode off.

A couple hours later, he was riding down the well-treed slope into the yard of the ranch house once owned by the late Ulysses Hungerford, head of the Buckskin County Cattlemen's Association.

Charlie McAllister looked up from where he was hanging a new door on the bunkhouse to Pike's left. "Brodie? Welcome, old friend." He wiped his hands off on his pants leg and held one hand out.

Pike dismounted and shook hands. "Looks like you're doin' well, Charlie."

McAllister caught something odd in the bounty hunter's voice. "Reckon I am. That bother you? I thought you'd be happy for us."

"Well, I am."

"But...?

"How'd you come by this place?"

McAllister's eyes narrowed in anger. "I don't think that's any of your concern, Brodie."

"It is, Charlie. I promised Hungerford's widow, who thought you or one of the others would come and squat here, that if you did, I'd put a stop to it."

McAllister smiled in relief. "We ain't squatters, Brodie. You should know better than that. We bought this place fair and square from the widow. Harland Barrington handled things for her. I think she's up in Cheyenne or something. Barrington owns the paper on it."

Pike nodded. "That's a relief to hear, Charlie. I had to make sure though."

"I understand."

"How'd you come by all the cattle? At least I figure you have a lot more than you did a few years ago."

"A hell of a lot more. We sold some of our cattle to buy a lot more head than that from the widow. She didn't care about price, and Barrington just wanted to be shed of everything. Miles Appleyard and Granville Forsythe tried to protest, but they had no real claim to the cattle, and after you scared the bejesus out of those two, they were happy enough to head for Texas or Montana Territory, or somewhere. Finally, Barrington just sold us the whole damn herd for pennies a head just to be shed of 'em. Holds the paper on them too, but that's almost taken care of after we sold a bunch at market last year."

"You keep 'em all?" Pike asked, surprised.

"Hell no. You should know better than that too. I

kept the largest number, but all the rest of the families got a good share, Connor the most."

"How're you carin' for 'em all?"

"My sons, Matt and Able, you remember them?" When Pike nodded, McAllister continued, "They're a big help. Floyd Dunn and Arch Blake are here too. All the boys stay in the bunkhouse."

"Even yours?"

McAllister grinned. "Yep. Figured it'd teach 'em some humility."

"It should."

The rancher finished with the door, then said, "Come on, Brodie, let's get your horse cared for and head inside. Supper should be ready soon. Viv'll be excited to see you."

"And Marcy?" Pike asked cautiously.

"She's been mighty subdued since you left. She's being courted by Vin and Matt Foley. Friendly rivalry, mostly, between the brothers. I ain't sure how she'll react to your visit, I surely ain't."

"Well, I'd hate to upset her. I'll move on if you think that's best."

"Nope. You're a friend, and the man I owe all this to." He waved his hand around, taking in the house, outbuildings, and the pasturage beyond. "She gets upset, she'll have to deal with it. Viv'll take care of it if need be."

They tended to Pike's sorrel and headed for the house. As they walked up the steps to the porch, McAllister called, "Viv. Viv, looks who's here."

"Quit your hollering," Viv McAllister said as she pushed open the door. A grin spread across her still-handsome face. "Brodie!" She hugged him and even gave him a peck on the cheek. "You're looking good for an old saddle tramp."

"Hah! And you're lookin' good for a beautiful woman who's had to live with this fella," Pike responded with a smile, chucking a thumb at McAllister.

"Well, if you two are done spoonin' with each other, let's go inside," McAllister said, but he grinned widely.

Marcy McAllister, Charlie and Viv's now nineteen-year-old daughter, stood stiffly by the dining room table. She made no move to come toward Pike, but said, "Welcome back, Mr. Pike."

"Thank you, Miz Marcy." He was about to say more, though he was unsure what, so he kept silent at a small nod from Viv.

Supper was something of a strained affair when Viv asked, "What've you been up to all this time, Brodie?"

"Been here and there, done this and that."

"But you…"

"Now ain't the time, Viv," McAllister said quietly.

The rest of the meal was eaten in silence. When it was over, the two men headed outside and plunked themselves in rockers, coffee in hand, enjoying the mountain's cool evening.

"There's more to you going here and there and doing this and that, Brodie," McAllister said after a few minutes. "You don't want to talk about it, I understand. But I'm interested and would like to hear what your life's been like since you saved all our bacon here."

"It's…"

"I'd like to hear too," Viv said, pouring more coffee for the men, then settling into another chair.

"Well, most of it ain't interestin', and some of it's downright awful."

"We've heard—and been through—awful things before, Brodie," Viv said quietly. "I reckon you didn't come here to talk about things, but a woman's intuition tells me you want to, or maybe just should, and speak your piece. Might be good for you."

"Well, after I left here," Pike started slowly, eyes staring out into the growing darkness, "I really did ride about here and there. Then got mixed up in a fracas down in Arizona Territory. Did some awful things that…well, I ain't ashamed of doin' even though they were awful, but I am ashamed that I was duped into doin' 'em. Ain't the first time I've been made a fool of, but I decided it ought to be the last. So I headed up here into Colorado Territory, just wanderin' aimlessly. Then I found me a beautiful meadow that I thought would make a fine home. It was away from people so I couldn't get in trouble or cause it for people."

"You don't cause trouble for people, Brodie. You just don't," Viv said.

Pike offered a crooked smile. "Nearest place was Skeeter Creek, a boomin' minin' town four days ride from where I was. A closer town had gone under not long before. Anyway, I built myself a nice little adobe house. Well, maybe it wasn't all that nice, I ain't much of a builder. While I was buildin' it, some Utes come along. They were about ready to throw me off their land but decided to let me stay. I became friends with 'em, especially Blind Bull and his son, Crazy Hawk." His voice grew faint, as if coming from far away. "And I met Bull's daughter, Hawk's sister, a woman named Little Raven."

"You cohabited with an Indian woman?" Viv gasped.

"Shocking, ain't it? You may not want to believe it, but she was a fine woman. Carin', helpful, lovin'. Beautiful too."

"You found some preacher to marry a white man and an Indian woman?" Viv asked, incredulous.

"No, Viv, we married Ute style. No real ceremony, we just took up life together mostly."

"That's sinful, absolutely..."

"That's enough, Viv," McAllister said sharply.

"But..."

"It ain't our place to judge, Viv. I expect love don't come in the way we expect it sometimes, and it's obvious to anyone who hears him that he loved this woman."

"Thanks, Charlie." Pike was silent for a while before he continued. "I used to go to Skeeter Creek now and again for supplies. On my way one time, I came up on some men—white men—abusin' an old Ute and his equally old squaw. They were doing things no man..." Pike stopped for a moment. "I knew I shouldn't get involved. They were just a couple of Indians."

"But they were old people," Viv said, suddenly

outraged that people—any people—could be treated in such a way. "Helpless."

"But they were just Indians, Viv. Just Indians."

"That doesn't mean..." She clamped her mouth shut, then said, "I understand."

"Well, I disabused those four men of the notion that this was a good way for men to behave."

"They won't do anything like it again, will they?" McAllister said more than asked.

"No. But by my helpin' 'em, I caused trouble. You see the folks of Skeeter Creek didn't take too kindly to the notion of me killin' four white men to protect a couple of old Indians."

"So they arrested you?" McAllister asked.

"Nope. But sometime later, they attacked Fallen Timber's little village. That was the old fella's name. Slaughtered everyone there but two, a mother and her eleven-year-old daughter. I rode like hell hopin' to save them, but..." He gritted his teeth as the remembrance brought back the rage he felt. "I found the girl on the side of the trail. She was abused far beyond what anyone could think men could do to a child."

Even in the growing darkness, Viv could see tears in Pike's eyes. She reached over and gripped her husband's arm tightly.

"I wanted to try to get her back to her people to get help, but I knew she..." He choked to a stop. "She begged me to send her to the Spirit World, to let her soul be free. There was nothing I could do. So...so, I killed her. She looked at me in shock for a moment, then smiled. Lord Almighty, I killed that poor girl." His voice was choked and full of despair.

"Oh, dear Lord," Viv said. She rose and knelt at the side of Pike's chair. She took one of his hands and held it to her cheek, letting him feel her tears that she freely shed, unlike him. "You did right, Brodie. Painful as it was. You did right. No girl should suffer so. How could men do such a thing? To a little girl?" She looked up at Marcy.

The girl had been listening at the door and had come out. She placed a hand gently on Pike's shoulder. She was too shocked to cry.

Pike patted Marcy's hand, then squeezed Viv's. "Thank you, ladies. Now go on back to where you were."

Viv took her seat, but Marcy stayed where she was.

Pike took a deep, deep breath and eased it out. "The Bible says, 'Vengeance is mine sayeth the Lord.' But not this time. No, this time it would have read, 'Vengeance is mine sayeth Brodie Pike.' I take no shame at all in the gruesome manner I paid back those men."

"Whatever you did to them, Brodie, it wasn't bad enough," McAllister said.

CHAPTER TEN

"What happened then?" Viv asked.

"Well, I figured once again that it was time for me to mosey on. I didn't want to cause the Utes anymore trouble." He smiled. "But Little Raven wouldn't let me go. I tried to leave, but she found me and told me she'd follow me where I went, no matter how difficult things might be. I was her man, she said, and she was my woman, and she belonged with me. The fool."

"Smart woman," Viv insisted.

"So I moved into the village with her. Lasted more than a year, but I got the itch to move on. I was planning to leave her again, but damn—pardon me—if she didn't force me to take her."

"So where is she now?" Marcy asked almost cheerfully.

"Dead," Pike said flatly as the two women gasped.

"More white men, I suppose," McAllister said.

"Nope. Utes. They found us and didn't like a Ute woman being with a white man."

"Didn't they know you?"

"No. Different band far removed from Blind Bull's group. I buried her and paid those Utes back in kind."

"Good thing too," Viv said.

"Ya know, Brodie," McAllister said, "it ain't you that causes trouble. You try to stop trouble. But trouble keeps comin' along kickin' you in the rump. And when that happens, you have to go fix it up as best you can."

"I wish that were true, Charlie." He sighed again. "I'm sorry folks that you had to hear that. I didn't mean to say so much. It just kind of boiled up and out. It was wrong of me to pour out such grief and horrors to the likes of you two ladies."

"That's all right, Brodie," Viv said. "I'm glad you did. It only reinforces my belief that you are a good man. Only man I know who is better is Charlie McAllister, and he's better in a different way."

"Bah." He patted Marcy's hand again and looked up at her over his shoulder. "Now ain't you glad your folks stopped you from traipsin' after me?"

"It's probably better," the young woman said, "but I can't say as I'm glad about it."

Pike shook his head.

"Why don't you two ladies go on back inside and clean up, get ready for bed." When the two had gone inside, McAllister asked, "So, why are you here, Brodie? I reckon it wasn't to tell us those horrors."

"No, it sure wasn't. Didn't mean to. And I'm damned ashamed that I did." He sighed once more. "But it's too late to take it all back."

"So, what is it?"

"You've seen that special Sharps I carry."

"Sure. I've never seen another like it."

"It's a hell of a weapon, and I've carried it and cared for it for a long time."

"I know that."

"And it's stood me in good stead."

"I know that too. Brodie, what's this all about?"

"It was stolen not long ago. I got it back but as I was leavin' Denver, I realized it might be time to stop carryin' it with me all the time. So I was hopin' to impose on you to keep it for me."

"What am I gonna do with it?"

"I mean just hold it for me. Put it up safe somewhere. If I ever figure I need it, I'll know where it is and that it's safe. I can just come by and get it."

"Figurin' it'll get stolen again?"

"Not really. But carryin' it around is getting to be too much trouble. If I want it to be effective, I have to worry about carin' for it, and when it's bangin' around on the side of the horse much of the time, well, that's no way to treat it."

"But why me? Why here?"

"You're the only one I'd trust with it."

McAllister was taken aback a little. "You sure?"

"Yep. Look, Charlie, I don't have much in the way of real friends. You're the closest I got to one. I come to respect you a lot during your troubles a few years ago. For a man not used to such doins, you were strong and steadfast in the face of those difficulties."

"Now you're startin' to embarrass *me*, Brodie," McAllister said, not wanting to look at his companion.

"Good," Pike said, suddenly laughing. "I bet Viv'll be happy to see you with a red face when you take to bed tonight."

"Oh, shut up, Brodie." But the rancher smiled.

"It's all true, though, and why I'd trust you with a weapon that's special to me."

"Sounds like a real responsibility," McAllister said, a grin twitching the corners of his mouth. "I'll have to think some on it."

"Well, take as long as…"

"Okay, enough thought." The grin broke out full. "Of course I'll do it, Brodie. Hell, if I said no and Viv heard about it, I'd never be sharin' her bed again, red face or not. And like as not, I'd go hungry most days."

"Viv is a strong woman, that's for certain. Ain't many like her." Pike's face grew wistful.

"I bet that Ute woman of yours—Little Raven, you said—was a lot like Viv," McAllister said quietly.

"Yep, she was. Feisty but lovin'. Wouldn't take no guff and sassed me whenever she felt I needed it. Which is often." Pike laughed, the melancholy slipping away.

"Alas, that's true with me and Viv too. But she's stuck with his ol' boy through it all, good times, bad times, raisin' kids, the troubles we had with Hungerford and the others, all of it. Never gave up on me." His voice had grown wistful but was quickly back to normal.

A voice floated out from inside the house. "I'll remember you said that, Charlie." It was followed by a hearty chuckle.

"And through it all she's been an annoyance,"

McAllister said with a laugh. "If she weren't such a good woman, a beautiful woman, a good cook, a good mother, hell, a good everything, I would've left her years ago." He laughed again. "All right, Brodie, go get that fancy rifle of yours. I think I got just the right spot for it."

Before long, the rifle, still in its scabbard and wrapped in a thick buffalo hide, was resting in a secret nook behind a bookcase the family did not use. "Anyone else know about this hidey-hole?" Pike asked.

"Viv. No one else. At least not that I know of. I'll keep good watch on it, Brodie, just in case. And knowin' how much it means to you, I'll horsewhip anyone who touches it, includin' Marcy or even Viv."

"I don't know as if I'd like you to go that far, Charlie, but I like the sentiment."

"Now, how about a snort or maybe two before headin' for some shut-eye."

"Sounds good."

* * *

"I hope you're plannin' to stay a while, Brodie," Viv said the next morning at breakfast.

"A day or two at most, Viv. It's time I got back to work. I took care of some business up north, and then took the time to pay my last respects to..." his voice faded, then returned to normal "...Little Raven. I was headin' back to takin' care of more business when I decided to come here for something."

Viv looked at him in question.

"I asked Charlie to keep something for me, hide it away."

"Something bad?" The woman didn't seem at all concerned.

Pike smiled, "Nope. Just something important to me that I don't need anyone else gettin' his hands on."

"The ri—" She stopped at Pike's look and nodded.

"What're you talkin' about?" Marcy asked.

"No concern of yours, child," Viv said.

"I'm not a child anymore, Ma."

"You're right, Marcy. I'm sorry." She smiled softly. "Sometimes it's hard for a mother to admit that her baby is a grown woman. Makes a mother feel old."

"Oh, Ma, you ain't old. Pa on the other hand, he's..."

"You finish that sentence the way I think you are, girl, and I'll have you cleanin' my boots after I get back from inspectin' the cattle."

Marcy stuck her tongue out at him, and they all laughed.

* * *

Pike liked his stay around the McAllister, Felder, and the other small ranches. He was greeted well by everyone. Even Becca Felder melted a little and invited him to supper, a strained affair at first but one that eased considerably when Becca realized that Pike was not in the area to recruit her husband for any other foolhardy adventures.

Even the children liked him, specially two girls and a boy, all around eight or nine. They seemed fascinated by his guns though scared a bit by his hard look—until he smiled and played with them a little.

It was the children who had him thinking that maybe he could settle down. The people here knew him and accepted him. He wasn't sure he could become a ranch hand, but it might be worth a try. Still, he was not ready to make such a momentous decision.

He was giving it serious consideration while he shaved one morning in a washroom in McAllister's house. He almost cut himself when he heard a short screech and cranked his head around to see Marcy standing in the doorway, staring.

He turned as Viv suddenly appeared and grabbed her daughter by the arm. "You should know better, girl," she snapped. She looked up. "I'm sorry, Brodie." She stopped and then gasped as she got a good look at his naked chest, "My God, Brodie."

Pike set the razor down and grabbed his shirt. "Ain't very pretty is it, Viv?" he said as he donned the garment.

"No, it ain't. I knew you'd been shot before and all, but Lord Almighty, Brodie, how have you survived?"

"A strong constitution and an ornery disposition. But mostly luck. Now you two best run along. I'll be out for breakfast in just a bit." Before long, he was at the table. As soon as he sat, he said, "I'll be leavin' as soon as I finish eatin', Charlie."

McAllister looked surprised.

"You don't have to leave, Brodie, just because Marcy and I..."

"Did he try to do something wrong with Marcy?

Or you?" McAllister demanded. He was scared down to his toes. He knew he could never take Pike in any kind of fight, but he knew he had to protect his wife and daughter.

"Of course not, Charlie. You should know better than that. Brodie would never do anything to shame either of us." She paused. "Have you ever seen him without his shirt on?"

"No, of course not. What kind of question is that?"

"Marcy and I did a few minutes ago. He was shaving and had his shirt off. The man is full of holes. Front and back. Bullet holes. Healed up, maybe, but bullet holes. And maybe some old scars from knife wounds. Marcy saw it first, then me when I went to get her."

McAllister looked at his daughter. "This true?" he asked quietly.

"Yes, Pa," she answered, head hanging.

"Brodie," Viv said, "There's no reason to leave. Marcy and I were shocked, still are, I reckon. Marcy's likely more upset than I am. She might even be scared as well, but she'll get over it. Neither of us are worse for knowing you. We care about you, Brodie, very much, and this doesn't make a tick's worth of difference. What shocked us most is that you've endured such things. No man should have faced so many bullets. We're sorry for you, Brodie. We're sad that you've been hurt so bad. And there's no way on God's earth that we would turn you away because of what we saw today." Tears were running slowly down her cheeks. "You're almost kin to us, Brodie. Please stay."

"I'm obliged, Viv, but what just happened only

proves to me that I can never settle down. Not among decent folks, anyway. No, ma'am, it's time for me to move on, to do what I do despite the dangers." He offered a crooked smile. "And the bullets."

"But..."

"Enough, Viv," McAllister said quietly.

"You don't mind him leaving?"

"I do. I wish he'd stay as much as you do. I don't believe that he can't settle down among decent folks. But *he* believes it. Maybe someday he'll find another woman who'll treat him as good as Little Raven did and settle down. And I purely hope that if that does happen that he will settle down among us. He wouldn't even have to work. As much as he's done for us, he can sit on his rump all day and have the rest of us do his biddin'."

"I didn't do much, Charlie."

"Like hell," he said without reprimand from either woman for his profanity. "If it weren't for you, most of us'd be dead and the rest driven off in poverty, without a roof over our heads or a pot to piss in. Despite all that, you ain't about to listen to reason, not from me, and not from these two women."

"He's right, Brodie," Viv said. Then she sighed. "About all of it, not the least the part of not listening to reason. And I also ask that if you ever do settle down do it here among us. If you never meet the right woman, then maybe when you get old enough that you can't do what you do for work, and if you don't get killed, then retire here with us."

"Please, Brodie," Marcy added.

"You'll be married soon, and I don't think your husband'd like a fella like me around."

"To the devil with him, whoever he might be."

"Marcy!"

"Hush, Mama. It's true, and I reckon you feel the same."

Viv could think of nothing to say to that.

"I can't promise anything, but if I ever decide to give up bounty huntin' for whatever reason, I'll come back here. But I'll likely bring trouble with me."

"Stop with this bringin' trouble nonsense, Brodie," McAllister said.

Chapter Eleven

Pike was not surprised when he rode through Graystone and saw that the headquarters of the Buckskin County Cattlemen's Association had lost a considerable amount of its grandeur. It was now a restaurant and saloon of a somewhat lesser clientele.

But he did not linger, just rode on through and kept going, heading north.

A few days later, he rode into Denver. He went straight to the county sheriff's office and checked with the lawman, Noah Devlin. From Devlin he learned that Ben Sykes and his gang had robbed a bank in Middle Boulder again and one in Gold Hill, then one in Boulder.

"Looks like I'm heading northwest, then," Pike said.

"Good hunting. I hope you find 'em. Tell the truth, I'd as soon see 'em come back across a saddle as sittin' on one."

"I'll keep that in mind." He paused.

Pike headed out. Something about Devlin bothered him but he could not put a finger on it. He shoved it to the back of his mind, stabled his horse, got a room in a less-than-grandiose hotel, and finally drifted into a restaurant, where he chowed down on chicken and dumplings, peas, and biscuits. Sated, he wandered around the city before strolling to the Mountain Goat.

An hour later, he left. Dark had settled over the city as he walked down the main street. Suddenly someone slammed him on the back of the head. He stumbled a few steps, then fell on hands and knees into an alley. Groaning, he fought off the blackness and struggled to rise while trying to draw one of his pistols. But he fell back on his rump, vaguely aware that someone was moving toward him. "Damn," he muttered as he attempted to get his hands to work right. But he finally managed to get a Colt out and fired as the face neared him and hands reached out for him.

The blast was bright in the dark alley, and when it faded a moment later, the person had turned and was hurrying off. Pike shoved himself gingerly and holstered his Colt. The world swirled before him and he reached out a hand to steady himself against a wall.

Moments later, someone silhouetted at the alley's opening, asked, "You all right, Mister?"

"Think so."

"What happened?" A man walked a step into the alley.

"Someone whacked me on the head. Reckon he was aiming to rob me."

"Happens a lot, Mister. Doc Bailey's place is two blocks down the street on the corner of Halladay Street."

"Thanks."

"You need help gettin' there?" The man didn't sound as if he wanted to help.

"I'll be all right."

The man left but a minute later, he was replaced by another. "It's Marshal Groves, Mister. Who're you?"

"Name's Brodie Pike."

"The bounty hunter?"

"Yep. Don't feel like much of one right now. Damn."

"Everybody faces trouble at one time or another."

"True. I've faced a hell of a lot worse than this, Marshal. Still, I feel like a fool to have been caught like this."

"Come on, let's get you down to the doc's."

He and Pike moved out of the alley and stopped when the bounty hunter said, "Ain't necessary. I just have a headache is all, and that'll go away soon enough."

"Your choice. If it was me, I'd see Doc Bailey. He might have some kind of powder or concoction that might help."

"I'll consider it."

Marshal Fred Groves looked suspiciously at him in the dim light of the streetlamp. "You see who did it?"

"Nope, it was too dark," Pike said after the briefest moments of hesitation. "Got hit from behind and fell in the alley, which is mighty dark, as is obvious."

"I heard a shot. Was that you?"

"Yep. Don't think I got him, though. It's dark here, too, but I don't see any blood. And though I was foggy, it didn't seem that he was havin' any trouble movin' when he took off."

Groves gave Pike a hard stare, then said, "I don't think you're bein' entirely truthful with me, Mr. Pike. I suspect you know damn well who it was and plan to go after him yourself."

The bounty hunter shrugged.

"Let me warn you, Mr. Pike, I won't countenance you or anyone else floutin' the law around here. You should let me know who did this and let me bring him to justice."

Pike shrugged again.

"If you try to mete out your own brand of justice, I'll come after you. This is my town, sir, and I'm the law here. I may not be the gunman you are, but I'll find you and try my damnedest to make you pay for what you did in such a case."

"Could be dangerous."

"I know that. So's drinkin' more than two small glasses of rotgut in the Mountain Goat."

Pike stared at the lawman for a minute, then chuckled. "Glad I only had one." He paused. "You sound like an honest lawman."

Groves grinned a little. "Are there any other kind?"

"Well, to be honest, I've known a few who didn't live up to that expectation."

The marshal sighed. "There are too many of those

I'm afraid. Well, can I escort you back to your hotel? Make sure someone doesn't come back to finish what he started."

"I believe you just want to keep a watchful eye on me, Marshal Groves. Something an honest lawman would do."

"You found me out."

"Then let's go."

When they arrived at the hotel, Groves said, "I warn you, Mister Pike, do not try to take justice into your own hands."

"I won't try anything tonight. You have my word."

"And beyond tonight?"

"I'll have to think on that once my head clears up some."

"I don't like the sound of that, but there's not much I can do about it 'til you try something. Though I expect I could find something to charge you with and toss you in the hoosegow for a few days."

"That, too, would be dangerous."

"I expect it would. Is it necessary?"

"Not for tonight."

"Can I trust you?"

"You may not know me, Marshal, but I am a man of my word. Once I give it, I stick to it unless some extraordinary events force me to reconsider."

The lawman looked at him for a few moments, then nodded. "Good night, Mr. Pike."

"And to you, Marshal."

* * *

Pike's head still throbbed as he headed to the sheriff's office in the morning, before breakfast. He was a little surprised to see Noah Devlin at his desk but was glad of it.

"What can I do for you, Mr. Pike?" Devlin asked sounding a bit nervous to Pike.

"I meant to ask yesterday. You got any fresh paper on Sykes? Maybe something with a newer drawin' of him?"

"Don't think so but let me check."

While the lawman was rummaging through some papers on his desk, Pike surveyed the room. His eyes narrowed when he saw Devlin's hat. But the sheriff turning around with a sheet of paper in his hand brought him back to attention.

"Not sure this drawin' of him is any better but it's the latest we got."

Pike took it, folded it, and put it in a shirt pocket. "Obliged, Sheriff." He headed to Sarpy's restaurant for breakfast. He was enjoying his hen's eggs, fresh-made sausage by an old German butcher in town, biscuits, and coffee when Groves tossed his hat on the table and plunked down in a chair across the table from the bounty hunter.

"You always welcome yourself to someone's table when he's eating?" Pike asked, irritated.

"Well, I am the law and..." He stopped. "That's a load of manure, ain't it?" Without waiting for an answer, he said, "I apologize, Mr. Pike. It was rude of me. Sometimes a fella forgets his manners. I'll speak to you later." He started to rise.

"Sit, Marshal."

Groves did and ordered coffee.

"No breakfast?" Pike was surprised.

"My wife makes a breakfast a lot better than anything you'd get here."

"One of the many benefits of being married, I suppose."

"Have you ever...?" Groves shut up and sipped some coffee. "You think of anything new about last night?"

"Nope."

"How long you plan on being in Denver?"

"Few days, maybe. 'Til my head clears up."

"I thought you were hot on the trail of some outlaws."

"Where did you hear that?"

"Didn't hear it. Just figured it would be true. I figure a man like you is always hot on the trail of some outlaws."

"More often than not the trail is cold, really cold," Pike said wryly.

"You plannin' on doing anything I should be concerned about while you're here?" The lawman's voice had a harsher tone to it.

"Ain't you supposed to be out on the streets of this fine city keepin' it safe from miscreants?" Pike countered.

"That's what I'm doin' in here, Mr. Pike. Like I told you last night, I can't have some gunman wanderin' around Denver takin' justice into his own hands while I'm here. Now, if you tell me you won't do anything, I'll believe you." He smiled. "'Course I might just keep an eye on you at times, but I believe you when you said once you give your word you keep it."

"I can't do that, Marshal."

"That's too bad. I'll tell you now, though, that while you're here, I'll be on your tail like fleas on a dog."

"You can't watch me every minute, Marshal. You got other duties, as well as a family."

"That's my concern." He stood. "Enjoy your breakfast, Mr. Pike."

"I will." But he stared at the door for some time after Groves had left through it.

* * *

Pike spent the next few hours in his room, caring for his weapons and resting. The headache had eased considerably, though was still there when he left the hotel and headed to the marshal's office. He was glad he found Groves.

"How about I buy you lunch, Marshal?"

"I'd rather eat at home. Beatrice's likely waitin' on me." Then he saw the look on Pike's face. "But I reckon I can have one of my deputies run over there and tell her I have city business to handle. It is city business, ain't it?"

"Mostly."

The lawman looked at him quizzically but then had one of his deputies take his message to Mrs. Groves. "All right, Mr. Pike, let's go."

They ordered their lunches at Sarpy's and waited

'til they came. As they started to eat, Groves asked, "So what's this about?"

Pike hesitated, then said, "I'm taking a risk here, Marshal. I told you last night that I think you're an honest lawman. I've thought that about a few others, and I've been wrong more than once, though I'm usually right."

"In my case you are," Groves said around a mouthful of pork chops.

"I think I am." He chewed on his beefsteak for a bit before saying, "I know who it was who attacked me, and I don't think you'll be happy when you learn who. And I ain't so sure you'll be able to do anything about it."

"Like I said, this is my town and I'm the law here."

"But it ain't your county."

Groves stopped with a forkful of chop halfway to his mouth. "What's that supposed to mean?" He shoved the food into his mouth.

CHAPTER TWELVE

"It's Sheriff Devlin," Pike said.

Groves almost spit out the mouthful of food. "You sure?" he finally sputtered.

"Yep. I saw him last night. I was foggy but I was sure it was him. When I fired, I caught a glimpse of him in the muzzle flash, and I thought I put a slug through his hat. I did. I saw the hat this mornin' in his office. Nice little hole in it."

I see what you mean about this being a troublesome thing. I ain't happy with learnin' it was him, of course. He puts a blight on every good lawman. But I'm not sure what I can do. Though I am the city marshal, and he is in the city, so I suppose he's in my jurisdiction."

"Could be tricky for you and hazardous to your career."

"That's a fact sure as anything." He sighed. "Well, I'll have to think on this. And I'd be obliged if you'd keep this to yourself. And don't do anything 'til I'm ready."

"Which might be never."

"Might. If that looks like the case, I'll let you have a free hand."

"Let me?" Pike asked with raised eyebrows.

"You know what I mean."

"Yes, I do. So I'll keep quiet as far as this goes." He paused. "Of course, if that son of a bitch tries again, which he might considering he missed his opportunity last night and might figure I know it was him, I'll put a bullet in him."

"I hope it doesn't come to that."

"Me too." He smiled at Groves's look of surprise. "I don't kill people for the hell of it. I ain't afraid of killin' and I'm damned good at it, but I only do it when necessary, like when I'm threatened or a little girl is..." He tossed down his fork. "Excuse me, Marshal." He stomped out leaving a thunderstruck Groves sitting there agape.

The next afternoon, Pike was sitting in the Plains View saloon, as usual with his back facing the wall, when Groves came in. The lawman looked around, not making any sign that he saw Pike. He had a shot of rotgut, then headed toward the bounty hunter's table. He ignored Pike as he passed by, but he surreptitiously dropped a piece of paper on the table.

Pike, who had enough sense to not acknowledge the lawman, slid his hand across the wood surface of the table, gently placed a palm over the paper and slipped it toward him. He glanced around, his seat giving him a view of the entire room and saw Groves talking to several townsmen at another table. Another quick scan showed him that no one was paying him any heed. He flipped the paper over and, leaving it lying on the table, read it. *Meet me behind Calvert's feed store an hour after dark. Probably don't need to say this but make sure you ain't followed.*

Pike crumpled the paper and shoved it in a pocket. Minutes later, the lawman sauntered out. Pike lingered, sipping on a beer and partaking of the various, highly salty food set out for the taking at one end of the bar. After an hour, he too, strolled out and stopped on the boardwalk just to the right of the door. Dusk was fast approaching. Even more wary than usual, he wandered down to the livery stable along Cherry Creek near Holladay Street and took his time checking over his sorrel.

"Something wrong, Mr. Pike?" Alf Quaid asked.

The bounty hunter turned to the livery owner and smiled.

"Nope, Alf. Just lettin' the poor beast know I'm still around lest he forget just who rides him regularly."

Quaid chuckled. "Most horses don't forget. At least the good ones don't, and that gelding of yours seems like a mighty good one. Still, never hurts to let 'em know you're still around and care for it." Still chuckling, the liveryman walked away.

He left after half an hour or so, and then meandered along behind the buildings following the creek until he reached the rear of the feed store not far from Lawrence Street. He wanted to be early in case Groves had set a trap for him. He leaned back against a shed in the shadows created by the feebly glowing gas lamp near the corner of the shed and waited.

Before long the marshal shuffled up, warily searching around.

"You alone?" Pike asked from his position.

"Of course I am, dammit." Agitation coated Groves's voice. Then he added, "Ah, hell, concerned about a trap are you." It was a statement, not a question. "I would be too. I am alone."

Pike stepped out of the shadows. "So what've you got to tell me, Marshal?"

"I saw Devlin this mornin' as I was makin' my rounds. Had a nice hole in one side of his hat. Didn't say anything, of course, just greeted him like I usually do. I don't think he suspects I suspect him."

"All right, you believe me. What now?"

"I've had my suspicions about Devlin for almost as long as he's been sheriff of Jefferson County."

"You know anything?"

"Nope. Just a feelin'. He seems shady to me, like he's always schemin' or something."

"From the few minutes I've spent with him, I believe you. But you still haven't answered me. What now? I don't have much law learnin', so I ain't sure a city marshal can arrest a county sheriff."

"I ain't sure either, but I think I'm probably gonna find out soon."

"What'll county officials say?"

"Most of 'em don't like Devlin. A few think he's fine, and they might cause a stink. My concern about them is that they'll warn Devlin."

"That wouldn't be good."

"No, no it wouldn't. There's also the problem in that they just can't fire him if they wanted to do so. He's been elected, not appointed like I've been."

"But if he's been arrested?"

"We don't know. Just like we don't know if I even can arrest him. The city's lawyers don't know either." He sighed. "Another problem is that some of the county fathers aren't all that fond of you."

Pike was not all that surprised, but still asked, "Why? I haven't caused any trouble here."

"I know that and so do most of those men. But you're a bounty hunter, which to some of them means a man hunter—a man killer. Plus, you're a stranger here, not someone who lives in the city or even on one of the farms or ranches outside it."

The two were silent for a bit before Pike said, "The way I see it, Marshal, we have two choices, since there's so much uncertainty about all this. One, I ride out of town, which would make your job easier and probably be a relief to the county commission-ers. Trouble with that is, I ain't about to run, espe-cially from some snake-humpin' manure pile like Devlin."

"Or?"

"Or, I could take care of Devlin and *then* ride out of town. He'd be taken care of and I'd be out of your hair. Commissioners ought to be happy about it, too, especially the ones who think he's no good."

"Killin' him seems to be a mighty harsh penalty for hittin' you over the head."

"Well, there had to be a reason to do it."

"Maybe he just wanted to rob you. Some bounty

hunters carry a fair amount of money. Or so I've heard."

"True, sometimes. Could be that, though I got the impression he was aimin' to kill me before I got a shot off. If he was, there's a lot more reason than tryin' to rob me."

"Maybe he thought you were after him and he was goin' to kill you to silence you."

"That could be," Pike mused. "Maybe I'm just tryin' to make more of it than is really there so I can justify killin' him, at least to myself."

"You know I'd have to try to stop you."

"Yep," Pike said, a touch of sadness in his voice. "But you'd not be able to, unless you shot me in the back, and you sure as blazes ain't the kind of man to do that."

"I'd still have to try."

"I know. One of the hazards of being an honest lawman. That is a mighty big dilemma for me, Marshal. I have a choice between walking away from a man who knocked me on the head and maybe planned to kill me or killin' a good man, which is something I do not want to do."

"Would it really be so bad for you to just ride on?"

"Being the kind of man I think Devlin is, he'd be gloatin' how he run this great bounty hunter out of his town. Word would spread, and that would make my job of bringing in miscreants all the harder. It'd mean more killin' since outlaws would think I ain't so good and try to challenge me."

"I never thought of that."

"You never had to. It could also cause trouble for you."

"How's that?"

"Devlin hears that you tried to help me, and your life, or at least your job, won't be worth a duck's fart."

Groves paced a little before stopping in front of Pike again. "That puts a different light on things. I mean no insult to you, Mr. Pike, but the sullyin' of your reputation means little to me. My safety and my family's well-being are an entirely different matter."

"I'd feel the same way in your position." After a pause, he asked, "What about his deputies?"

"What about 'em?"

"Can any of 'em be trusted?"

"He's got five of 'em, three of 'em workin' in other cities around the county. The two left in town, I ain't sure of. I think Jones is pretty neutral and wouldn't mind seein' Devlin gone. Carter I don't know about. Why?"

"I thought that if one of them wasn't all that fond of his boss he might be willin' to help us come up with a plan to solve this. Doesn't seem like it."

There was some silence before Groves said, "I think I need a little more time to think this over. Maybe the city's lawyers will say I'm within my rights to arrest him."

"You're forgettin' something else, Marshal." When the lawman looked at him in question, Pike said, "What's he gonna face in court? An assault charge, maybe. No judge will be too upset by a county sheriff beltin' a bounty hunter over the head, especially if the lawman comes up with some reason for doing so, whether it's true or not. He'll most likely get fined, and it'll be a small one, I reckon."

"And that means my job, my family's well-being, and maybe even my life won't be worth a duck's fart, as you said. He'll be out to ruin me, if not kill me outright."

"Sadly, yes."

After some hesitation, Groves said, "You're a proud man, Mr. Pike. Anyone can see that. But so am I. And what I'm asking ain't easy for me. In fact, it's downright hard. Makes me ashamed of myself to be pleadin', but I ask you to ride out of Denver without killin' Devlin. If it was just me, I'd go after him at your side, but my family..."

There was some hesitation on Pike's part, but he finally said, "I'll ride out, Marshal. And I won't kill him. I ain't had much of a family in years, but I understand how important family can be. I'll need a day or two."

"Thank you, Mr. Pike...Brodie," Groves said in an almost whisper, his voice a little shaky.

"No need for thanks," the bounty hunter said and walked away.

CHAPTER THIRTEEN

Though he could not see them, Pike knew he was being watched by both city Marshal Fred Groves and county Sheriff Noah Devlin when he rode out of Denver early the next afternoon. He had had a good night's sleep, a decent breakfast at Sarpy's and then spent some time in Blake's mercantile, one of three in the city. He bought enough supplies to last a week, more if he was careful, and had them delivered to Alf Quaid's livery stable where he bought a mule and pack saddle. Quaid's helper aided Pike in loading the mule. Leaving the animal there, Pike strolled to a different restaurant—Gable's—for lunch.

Finally, he saddled the gelding, took the rope to the pack mule in hand and rode out of the city. When the afternoon sun began fading, the bounty hunter pulled into a stand of trees some yards off the road leading to Golden. He hobbled the sorrel and allowed it to drink and graze while he unloaded the mule. At last, he unhobbled his horse, mounted and, with the rope to the unburdened mule in hand, headed back to Denver.

It was well past midnight when he arrived, dismounted, and tied both animals to a hitching rail near Sheriff Devlin's house. In the darkness broken only by a half moon and a sky full of stars, he let himself in the unlocked back door of the lawman's house. He was glad the lawman lived alone. That way Pike wouldn't have to disturb a family, something he very much did not want to do.

Stealthily he moved upstairs and into Devlin's bedroom. He shook the lawman a little. "Wake up, Sheriff. Time to wake up."

"Who's that?" Devlin mumbled, swinging his legs around and placing his feet on the floor. "What's going on?"

As the sheriff rose, Pike whacked him hard in the forehead with one of Devlin's own revolvers, stunning him. Devlin was still mobile, though of clouded mind, which Pike wanted. The bounty hunter did not want to carry Devlin.

"C'mon there, Sheriff," Pike said almost gleefully.

"Where're we goin'?" Devlin asked in a slurred voice.

"And who're you?"

"You don't want to know." Pike grabbed the front of the lawman's long john shirt and tugged him forward, keeping the lawman's pistol in his other hand. They went down the stairs, Devlin stumbling all the way, and out the back door.

Standing next to the mule, the sheriff started to

come out of his fog a little and he looked at Pike, trying to figure out how he knew this man.

Pike shoved Devlin's pistol into the back of his own gun belt, pulled out a bandanna and gagged Devlin with it. Then he bent and lifted the lawman enough to flop him belly down over the mule's back. Pike swiftly tied Devlin down. He pulled out the sheriff's gun and lifted the lawman's head by the hair. "Ain't much fun being conked on the head is it?" he said just before clouting Devlin again, this time knocking him out.

Pike stuffed the pistol into a saddlebag, mounted the sorrel and, leading the mule, rode back the way he had come. It was well after dawn when he arrived back at his camp, and Devlin was awake. The lawman kept trying to shout imprecations, or at least that's what Pike figured he was doing, but could not because of the gag.

"Mornin'," Pike said almost cheerfully as he untied the rope holding Devlin on the mule's back. He used it to tie the lawman's hands behind his back, then dragged him off the animal onto his feet.

Devlin collapsed, his legs not working well after being tied for hours. Pike left him there as he unsaddled, tended, and hobbled the gelding. Done with that, he started a fire and put coffee on, then set bacon frying in a pan.

While those things were underway, Pike helped Devlin up and tied him, sitting, to a tree. Devlin's eyes bulged and the veins in his neck stood out as he tried to scream at Pike. The bounty hunter placed an index finger vertically across his lips and said, "Shh. You'll hurt yourself you keep this up." He went and had his meal, then carried some bacon and a cup of coffee to where Devlin was tied and knelt beside the lawman, whose eyes widened in anticipation.

Pike pulled the man's gag free, and the lawman began a rapid-fire, heated barrage of curses aimed at Pike. The bounty hunter shoved the gag back into Devlin's mouth. "You want some of this?" Pike asked, indicating the bacon and coffee.

Devlin nodded vigorously.

"Then you must be quiet when I remove the cloth. You get one chance. You say more than 'thank you' and you'll get nothing. Understand?"

Devlin nodded again. "Are you gonna untie..." He clamped his mouth shut at Pike's cocked eyebrow. "Thanks," he muttered.

Pike fed him. When Devlin was finished, Pike said, "If you think that now that you're fed you can start insultin' me, I should warn you that I do not suffer insults lightly. You keep your mouth shut and the gag stays out. Start spoutin' insults, and the gag goes back in."

"Can I ask questions?"

"Sure, if they're asked in a mannerly fashion." Pike went back to the fire and poured himself another cup of coffee.

"Why are you doing this?"

"As I said, I don't suffer insults lightly. I suffer attacks even less lightly."

"What attacks?"

"You can't be that foolish, Sheriff. I saw it was you when you clouted me over the head."

"I didn't…" He nodded.

"I'll turn your question back to you. Why did you do it?"

"You killed my brother. Well, half-brother."

"I've killed a lot of men, a lot more than I would've liked to. Who was he?"

"You didn't kill him directly. You brought him in, and he was hanged."

"What was his name?"

"Will Semple."

"Ah. Nice fella. Killed three people. Back in Kansas, I believe. Durin' a bank robbery."

"They were shootin' at him. What was he supposed to do?"

"Throw down his guns and surrender," Pike snapped.

"They would've killed him sure as hell."

"If he surrendered before he killed those people they might not have shot him. Likely just arrested him. He would've spent time in prison, but he'd still be alive."

"Maybe."

"Why didn't you just shoot me? I was almost out on my feet. Would've been easy to put a bullet in me."

"Would've drawn attention, like your shot did. If I had been caught, I would've ended up like my brother."

"It'd be well deserved."

"So what're you gonna do with me?"

"Ain't sure."

"You could let me go. It's a hell of a long walk back

to Denver, especially with me bein' barefoot and all. That'd give you plenty of time to get away."

"Nothing or no one to get away from really. Except you."

"I won't be comin' after you. My word."

"And I'm supposed to take your word? You're a bigger fool than I thought."

"I've heard you're a man not given to killin' for the sake of killin'. You kill me now and you'll be violatin' that code."

"Killin' a man who tried to send me to my just reward won't violate my code, if that's what you want to call it. And you had every intention of puttin' me in the grave."

"But I didn't."

"Only because you couldn't. You should have, though. Another shot at that time wouldn't have made any difference. You had killed me, no one would've given it a second thought—a county sheriff shootin' down a bounty hunter? No way the law would bother you over it. All you had to do would be to make up some story that I was tryin' to rob a bank or kill some innocent man believin' he was an outlaw."

"Damn," Devlin breathed.

"Didn't think of that, did you? Just got scared and ran. Just like that coward of a half-brother of yours."

"You son of a…"

"Now, now, watch your tongue, boy." He grinned a little. "Just sit tight while I load the mule. Don't want to leave all these supplies behind for some prospector or other traveler wanderin' by to find."

As he worked, Pike wondered what he should do with Devlin. It was not in his nature to just shoot the man down, though he felt that he would be justified in doing so. Besides, he had promised Marshal Grove that he would not kill the sheriff. There was also the quite real possibility that if he killed Devlin and was found out, he could have a bounty on his own head for killing a lawman. That would not do. There were times when he didn't care if he died, but this was not one of them.

He made sure the panniers were snug on the pack-saddle and went to saddle his horse. Letting Devlin go, he knew, would raise the same problems. The sheriff would make up some story of how he escaped the desperate man hunter and then sign out a wanted flyer on Pike. Pike swore silently at himself. This time he had brought on the untenable situation on himself, and he did not like that one bit. And he had no real answer to his problem.

"Well, damn," he muttered. He couldn't stay here, he figured. He got some rope and, leaving Devlin's hands tied behind his back, placed a slip knot around the sheriff's neck, then tied the rope to one of the pack saddle's forks. He looped the rest of the long rope around both front forks of the packsaddle. The lawman had enough room to walk side by side with the mule without bumping into the animal.

"Comfortable?" Pike asked sarcastically.

"Piss on you."

Pike moved off slowly, holding the rope to the pack mule. He went back to the main road, such as it was, but knew he couldn't stay on it long. There was too much of a chance of being discovered and explaining the situation would not be easy.

A mile farther on, he spotted a small trail off to his left and turned onto it. He figured it was on old prospectors' trail and likely would lead...somewhere. The trail began to climb upward, weaving among pines and boulders. It narrowed quite a bit as he rode, indicating it had not been used in some time.

Suddenly he stopped. Ahead, a tall, sharp cliff ran around to his left, leaving no passage. To the right was a fissure. He dismounted, tied the animals to a tree and went to investigate. The crack in the earth was maybe fifty feet deep with a string of jagged rocks at the bottom. "Well, I reckon this is why the trail ain't in the best of conditions," he mumbled.

Considering his options, he got a canteen and swallowed some water, then poured some into Devlin's mouth. The sheriff looked exhausted, and his feet were bleeding. Pike had little sympathy for him.

The bounty hunter hung the canteen back over the saddle horn, and he suddenly decided what to do. He unwound the long rope from the packsaddle and tied the end tightly to a weathered old pine. He freed the rope from where it tied the lawman to the animal and tugged the sheriff forward, stopping at the edge of the sharp drop-off.

"Wait, what the hell're you doin'?" Devlin asked, fear making his voice rise.

"You'll see," Pike snapped.

CHAPTER FOURTEEN

Pike took the slipknot off Devlin's neck and instead tied the rope around his chest and arms. Without a word, he kicked the legs out from under the lawman, who landed on his rump with a sharp exclamation. Pike pushed him to the edge, then grabbed the rope and shoved Devlin over.

The lawman screamed, but Pike had the rope and eased the sheriff down, down until Devlin dangled, screaming imprecations, twenty feet below the rim of the drop-off.

"Enjoy the view, Sheriff," Pike said. He turned, mounted the sorrel, and headed back down the thin trail. He stopped just before he reached the main road and had a meal of water and jerky. Then he was on the move again, turning north when he reached the main trail.

Less than two miles away, he spotted Marshal Fred Groves ahead of him, towing an extra horse. He closed the gap and from twenty yards away said, "Greetings, Marshal."

Groves stopped and sharply swung his head around.

"Where're you headed, Marshal?"

"Looking for you."

"Why?"

"Devlin's disappeared, and I thought you might have him."

"I left Denver alone. You were watchin', I figure."

"I was. Doesn't mean you didn't double back and grab him."

"Smart thinkin'. No wonder you're a lawman."

"Where is he?"

"Back there somewhere," Pike said, chucking his chin in the general direction of where he had left Devlin.

"I thought you said you wouldn't kill him."

"I didn't kill him."

"Then what…?" Confusion spread across Groves's face.

"Left him hangin' around an old trail back there a little way."

Groves stared at him for a minute or so, then said, "Take me to him."

"Can't do that, Marshal."

"Yes you can."

"So you can take him back to Denver? That wouldn't be so good for me."

"Why? You didn't really do anything to him. Did you?"

"Depends on what you mean. Doesn't matter,

though. You bring Devlin back to Denver and he'll try to see me dead or in prison."

"No, he won't."

"Don't be a fool, Marshal. He's been humiliated, and he's not a man to easily forget that. As soon as he can, he'll have paper out on me. Not only will I not be able to make my livin' in the world, but I'd be on the run from every lawman from the Indian Nations to Canada."

"I'll make sure he doesn't."

"I doubt you can."

"I can probably convince the commission to fire him, even if he is elected. Dereliction of duty or something. If he tried to send out paper on you, I'll squash it, and if he tries to telegraph other places, I'll have Pete send a fake telegram."

"Got it all figured out, do you?"

"Not all, no. But enough."

"And what if I don't take you to him?"

"Don't know," Groves said honestly. "I can't face you down in a gunfight and even if I could, it wouldn't work. If you kill me, I won't be going nowhere, of course. If I managed to kill you, you'd not be able to tell me where he is."

"Quite the dilemma."

"Yes, it is. Look, Mr. Pike, you told me you don't kill for the sake of it. I don't know what you've done with Devlin, but I figure he won't survive what you've done to him. Is it really necessary to kill him?"

"I think so. He tried to kill me."

"All he did was hit you on the head."

"He would've finished the job if I hadn't sent him runnin' off with a gunshot."

"Why would he do that?"

"He told me I had killed his half-brother. Well, I didn't but I brought him in and a judge hanged him. He still considers it me killin' him."

"I tell that to the commissioners and they'll find a way to get rid of him."

"You don't really believe that, do you?"

"I have to, Mr. Pike. As a lawman, I can't condone a man going out and killin' another lawman. It ain't in my nature."

"You have no jurisdiction here."

"True, but you grabbed Devlin in Denver, where I do."

Pike sat thinking. It could be a case where he tried to do something right—or at least save his hide from a man bent on killing him—but turn out bad if Groves pursued charges against him. On the other hand, it was assured that Devlin would do so if he got back to Denver. Still, leaving Devlin where he was amounted to almost the same thing as killing him in cold blood. Pike had reason to kill him, but either way, it could lead to trouble with him.

"Can I trust you, Marshal?"

"You should know the answer to that."

The bounty hunter nodded. "I'm putting my life in your hands. Keep that in mind." He turned and headed back down the road.

Almost two hours later, they arrived at the end of the road. Devlin must have heard them because he began screaming for help.

"You left him hanging there?"

"Yep."

"He would've died of exposure."

"Or his fussin' could have the rope scrapin' across the rock and eventually cut through it."

Groves blanched, then said indignantly, "Either way you would have killed him."

"Reckon you're right." Pike was unconcerned. "Can you pull him up by yourself, Marshal?"

"Reckon so. His horse'll help if need be."

"Like I said, Marshal, I'm puttin' my life in your hands." He tipped his hat and rode off. He didn't stop 'til after dark. He tended the gelding, unloaded the mule, hobbled the animals, and made a small fire. Soon he was eating bacon and some stale bread soaked in the grease, complimented by thick coffee. He soon turned in but had trouble sleeping.

He was grumpy in the morning as he ate and prepared the animals. It wasn't long before he was on the road, wanting to put as much distance as he could between himself and Sheriff Noah Devlin.

He stopped around noon for a quick meal of jerky and water and to let the animals feed, drink, and breathe. As he was tightening the cinch on his saddle, he felt ill at ease for some reason. That night, sleep did not come easy, and he knew why. "Hell, Brodie," he muttered into the night sky. "You know what you have to do."

In the morning, after breakfast, he loaded the mule, saddled the horse, mounted the gelding, and turned back down the road he had been following. He stopped the next night at the old prospectors' trail, then pushed on the next morning.

It was well after dark when he rode back into Denver having left the mule hobbled outside town. He carefully made his way to the back of Devlin's house. He was tying his horse to a loose board on the rear of a shed there when he heard something that seemed out of place. He drew a revolver and slid along the side wall to the front. No one was there, but the sound still was, and he realized someone was crying. It sounded like a woman. A bit of light showed through cracks in the shed's walls, and he peered through one of the cracks. He saw a woman tied in a wooden chair in the middle of the room facing away from the door. He could see no one else in the short field of vision he had.

As he considered going in to help the woman, his mind whispered, "Remember what happened last time you helped some people being abused by villains." Then he sighed. She was in trouble; he could not leave her there. He went around the corner and eased the door open, annoyed at the sound of the old, poorly nailed boards.

"Is someone there?" the woman asked, fear in her voice.

"Yes'm."

"Come to finish what your friends started." She sounded as if she were trying to choke back more tears.

"No, ma'am. I'm not one of the fiends who stuck you here. I'll get you out of here and get you to the safety of your home." He started to walk to her but stopped when she urgently asked him to in a frightened voice.

"Something wrong, ma'am?"

"Is there a blanket or something lying about? I think there's one on that bed in the back corner near you."

Pike looked around. "Indeed there is. It looks old but sturdy enough. I reckon it'll be enough to keep you warm 'til we get you away from here."

"I'm not cold." The words quavered into the air. She drew in a deep breath. "The...men, they..." More soft sobs broke out. "They cut away the bodice of my dress. I'm..."

"No need to say more, ma'am. I'll get the blanket and hand it to you over your shoulders. I won't look. You have my word."

"Thank you, Mister...?"

"Brodie Pike. And you are?"

"Beatrice Groves."

"Are you related to Marshal Groves?"

"I'm his wife."

It came as no surprise. "Do you know where he is?"

"You think he's abandoned me to the mercies of these beasts?"

"No, ma'am. I don't know your husband very well, but I know him well enough to know he would not desert you for any reason, and if he's at all able to do so, he'll be searching for you."

"Yes, that would be Fred. He's a most honorable man."

"Yep, he is." Pike edged forward until he was within

an arm's length of the back of the chair. "I'm gonna toss this blanket over your shoulder so I can cut these ropes holdin' you. I'll turn away as soon as you're free so you can cover yourself." He threw the blanket, and it landed half over her shoulder with more hanging over the back of the chair than her body. He knelt and quickly sliced through the ropes. As he stood, the blanket was pulled all the way over the chair.

"I know a blanket ain't the best thing for coverin' your modesty, but it'll have to do, and I suggest you do it swiftly. The sooner we get out of here the better."

Within moments, Beatrice stood. "Ready," she said nervously.

"I ain't about to stare but is it all right if I turn around."

"Yes." It was barely a whisper.

He turned and when he saw her, a large grin spread across his face. "I don't know much about women's fashion, Mrs. Groves, but I'd say you're the most stylish woman in Denver." Seeing the confused, shamed look on her face, he added, "My apologies, ma'am. I was trying to lighten such a dishonorable situation a tiny bit."

"Thank you for that, Mr. Pike. I'm ready to go."

"Have you ever ridden astride a horse?"

"I've hardly ever ridden a horse at all, but considering my ensemble, I think being astride a horse wouldn't be out of place."

Pike nodded. He went to the door and peeked out. Not seeing anything, he stepped outside. There was still no movement around. "All right, ma'am, come on."

The bounty hunter hurried the woman around to the back of the shed and helped her into the saddle. "Which way to your house, ma'am?"

"You're not going to ride, Mr. Pike?"

"Only way I could do that, ma'am would be to climb up there behind you, and you've been forced into enough immodesty for one night."

"Thank you again, Mr. Pike." She gave him directions. Walking alongside the horse's head, holding the reins, he moved as swiftly as was reasonable, which wasn't very swift at all, and it was an hour before they reached the house on Sixth Street.

As they walked, Pike asked, "Do you know where your husband is?"

"No," she said, her voice still heavy with worry and fear. "He walked me to the market and left me there saying he had to go meet with Sheriff Devlin. Two rough-looking men grabbed me and dragged me away while I was on the way home."

"Will you be all right at home? I can stay with you —outside, rather—if that would make you feel more comfortable. Of course, I wouldn't be able to look for the marshal that way."

"Do you think Fred is in trouble?"

"Yes ma'am, I do."

"Then find him, Mr. Pike. Find him and help him. Please."

"I will do so, ma'am." He helped her off the horse and watched as she hurried inside, the sounds of delight from her children escaping through the door for the few moments it was open.

The bounty hunter mounted the gelding. There were, he figured, two places where he likely would find Sheriff Noah Devlin. He checked the first place, the sheriff's office, which was closed. He rode to Hasting's saloon and tied the sorrel to a hitching rail. He cracked the saloon door open and saw his prey. He pushed inside, slamming the door and moving swiftly to one side and stood with his back only inches from the wall.

The slamming of the door brought everyone's attention to him.

CHAPTER FIFTEEN

"Well lookee here, boys," Sheriff Noah Devlin said with a grin. "Welcome, Mr. Pike. You coming here has saved us a lot of time trying to hunt you down. Or having others do it since you'd have had a price on your head."

Pike ignored him and quickly surveyed the room. Devlin and his two deputies sat at a table in the middle of the room. Five other men were scattered around the saloon. Marshal Fred Groves was tied to a post. Out of the corner of his eye he saw the bartender reaching for something under the mahogany bar. Without looking at him, Pike said, "You pull that scattergun like I figure you're doin', friend, and you'll get a bullet in the head. So reach down slowly, with one hand, and pick it up by the barrel." When the barman had done so, looking scared, the bounty hunter said, "Open it, pull out the shells and toss 'em in a corner, then lay the weapon down on the bar and move to the other end."

All the while, Pike had kept his vision on Devlin. He figured that no one would make a move without the sheriff's say so. When the bartender had done as he had been told, Pike said, "Let Marshal Groves go. He ain't done nothin' to you. It's because of him you're still alive."

"He's too friendly with you, and if I let him go, he'll be a nuisance. Of course, you'll be dead and the good old marshal here will be in as big a pickle as he is now." He grinned unctuously. "Besides, we want him nice and comfortable when we entertain ourselves with his wife. She's waitin' for us to go get her now. She should make for some good sportin' judgin' by what her naked bosom looks like. Quite delicious."

"You bastard!" Groves shouted.

"That wouldn't be very nice now, would it, Devlin?" The bounty hunter shrugged. "Well, no matter. You won't be around to do any sportin' with anyone." He glanced around the room. "Any of you boys don't want to get shot should clear out."

Devlin laughed. "You gonna shoot all of us?"

"If I have to."

"Think you're that good?"

"We'll find out. Besides, you'll be the first to go down. After that, these other boys might not think they'll want to stick around since their boss is ready for the boneyard."

One of the men started walking toward him. He glared at Pike but kept his hands away from his revolver. He stopped next to the bounty hunter. "Best watch your back, you son of a bitch," he snarled.

Without hesitation, Pike backhanded the man full in the mouth with the barrel of one Colt. The man staggered back, spitting out blood and teeth, then fell on his rump. Despite his wound, he had enough consciousness to reach for his pistol. Pike shot him in the stomach. He took two steps and stamped a boot heel on the man's forearm, snapping it, rendering it useless. He swung back to face the room.

And all hell broke loose.

The men began unlimbering their pistols. Pike ignored the bartender, who was heading fast for the back door, and fired at Devlin, who was moving, but missed. His next two shots, however, took out one deputy and another of the men. Two bullets tore through his shirt and another through his hat. Slugs whizzed by him, thudding into the wall behind him, and he jumped to the side, shoving over a table and ducking behind it. He didn't figure the flimsy piece of furniture would stop .44- and .45-caliber bullets in this small space, but he figured it was at least some little protection.

Pike poked his head and arm around the right side of the round table and fired twice. Two more gunmen went down but Pike wasn't sure whether they were dead or just wounded, but they were out of the battle for now. He switched Colts, popped up over the table and fired again. One deputy went down with a slug in his chest, and another gunman died with a bullet that had, with luck for Pike, shredded his throat.

The last two gunmen, firing wildly and hitting nothing, ran for the door, leaving only Devlin.

Pike stood. Not fearing Devlin's accuracy, he slid

away the Colt that still had three cartridges in it and began loading the other as he walked slowly toward the lawman.

The sheriff was wild-eyed. He pulled the trigger on his revolver again and again, but there were no live cartridges left. He dropped it, knelt, and grabbed another pistol.

Finished loading his six-gun, Pike shot Devlin in the chest. As the bounty hunter walked up to loom over him, the sheriff weakly tried to raise the revolver. Pike kicked it away.

"You'll never find the woman," Devlin whispered.

"He really has Beatrice, Brodie?" Groves asked, frantically struggling against the ropes holding him to the post.

"I sure do," Devlin said with a smug smile.

"No, he doesn't," Pike said. "She's home with her children, a little shamed perhaps by a state of dishabille but unharmed."

"You son of a bitch," Devlin gasped.

Pike grinned at him and began cutting Groves's bindings.

"You really mean it, Brodie? She's safe?" the marshal asked, using Pike's first name for only the second time.

"Yep. Found her a little while before I got here."

"How?"

"A couple of Devlin's boys grabbed her as she was headin' home from the market. You?"

"Same. Knocked me on the head and dragged me here."

Pike looked down at Devlin, who was still

breathing though it was labored. He drew a pistol to finish off the sheriff, but Groves stopped him. Pike's eyes narrowed. "I ain't lettin' you save this scum again, Marshal."

"Not gonna do that." He turned and spit on Devlin's face. "You are the lowest of the lowest, Noah. Lower than a snake's belly six feet underground. I should've let Mr. Pike leave you hangin' over that cliff." He picked up the pistol Devlin had planned to use and pulled the trigger. He got six clicks. "Empty too, dammit," he muttered. "Well, no matter." He suddenly slammed a boot heel down on Devlin's blood-covered chest.

The sheriff gasped, gurgled, then died.

Pike laid a hand on Groves's shoulder. "Time for you to get home and see to your wife, Marshal."

Groves nodded. Suddenly he asked, concern in his eyes, "You said dishabille?"

"Whoever grabbed Mrs. Groves cut her bodice off leaving her bosom…"

"Oh, dear Lord," Groves whispered. "Did you…?"

"No. She was tied to a chair facin' away from me. I tossed a blanket over her shoulder, cut the rope holding her and turned my back while she covered herself. I let her ride my sorrel while I walked alongside to your home."

"Thank the Lord." His eyes widened. "I'm sorry, Mr. Pike. Brodie. I didn't mean…"

"I know. Best get on home now. And I best be on my way."

"Oh, no you don't. It's well past dark, and you have nowhere to go at this hour." He grinned. "Besides, if I get home and tell Mrs. Groves what happened and I don't bring you with me, I'll be a dead man for sure."

"You don't need a man like me disgracin' your house, Marshal."

Groves's face clouded in anger. "I may have been joking about what Beatrice would do to me if I didn't bring you home, but I was not joking about having you in my home. Both me and Beatrice would be honored to have you *grace* our home."

"You certain?"

"I am."

"I think you're a fool for wantin' me to visit after all the trouble I caused you and your family."

"Trouble was bound to come up at some time with Devlin. Now, come on. I'm eager to get home."

They walked outside to see that a small crowd had gathered, drawn by the sound of gunfire.

"What's gone on?" someone asked.

"A little fracas, Burt. Nothin' you need be concerned about. But somebody go get the undertaker. He's gonna be busy tonight. And someone go get Commissioner Beales. Tell him there's been trouble with Sheriff Devlin and he's dead." He ignored the gasp from the crowd. "Tell Beales I'll explain everything in the mornin' and warn him to keep away from me 'til tomorrow. Same for the other commissioners and city council members. Now, let us through and then go home." He knew that would not happen but it sounded like something officious that a lawman would say. He and Pike pushed through the throng.

Since Groves had no horse here at the saloon, for

the second time that night, Pike walked along, holding the reins to the sorrel. As they walked, the bounty hunter said, "This may not be all over, Marshal."

"My name's Fred. And why do you say that?"

"Those two men who took off runnin' might think to come back and get revenge for their friends. If they were friends."

"You could be right. I'd wager they're still runnin', but I'll be on the watch."

"Look for 'em, Fred. Just don't watch for 'em."

Groves looked at Pike and saw that the bounty hunter was serious. He nodded.

Beatrice Groves screeched, first in fright when the door to her house opened, then in delight when she saw it was her husband. She rushed to him and threw her arms around him, hugging him tight and planting kisses all over his bearded face. Then over her husband's shoulder she saw Pike, who stood his face a mixture of warm humor and deep sadness.

"Oh, Mr. Pike. Thank you for bringing Fred home to us."

"I didn't do much, ma'am."

"The devil you say, I'd wager, lookin' at the two of you." She smiled, though her cheeks were red. "And as you can see, I'm presentable now."

Next to Pike, Groves stiffened a little.

"You were never not presentable, ma'am," the bounty hunter said. "Not that I could tell."

"Thank you, Mr. Pike." She smiled again, though still rosy cheeked.

Pike could tell that Groves relaxed.

"Are you two hungry?" Beatrice asked.

"Yes," both men answered in unison.

"I'll have something ready in minutes. Oh. where are my manners. How could I leave you still standing in the hallway? Come inside."

"In a moment," Groves said. "Billy, take Mr. Pike's horse to the livery. Wake Mr. Quaid and tell him I sent you. He's to take the best care of this animal."

"Yes, sir, Pa."

"Before you go, Billy, please bring in my saddle-bags and the Henry rifle. I'd be obliged."

"Take those things to the extra room, Billy," his mother ordered. "Mr. Pike will be spending the night with us as our guest."

"That's not necessary, ma'am."

Beatrice looked him square in the eye. "Yes, it is, Mr. Pike." Her voice said she would take no argument.

"Yes'm."

* * *

"That was a mighty fine breakfast, ma'am," Pike said in the morning. "And I'm mighty grateful for your hospitality, but it's time I was on my way."

"Oh, please stay another night or two."

"I'd like to but I have things to do, ma'am."

"Things like what?"

"Business," the bounty hunter said flatly.

"But what…"

"That's enough, dear," Groves interjected. A glance from him silenced any further questions she might have asked.

"Well, then, it's been a pleasure having you here.

And remember, you will always have a room here whenever you're in town. In fact, I'd be rather unpleased if you were to not stay here." She looked stern but blushed at the same time.

"You're right, Fred, she is a most formidable woman," Pike said with a straight face. "I don't know how you can stay married to her."

Beatrice's eyes widened and she turned an accusing look at her husband. A retort begged to get out of her mouth. Suddenly she laughed. "My Fred would never say such a thing, Mr. Pike. Even though it's true what you said about me."

The two men joined in the laughter. "Excuse my language, ma'am, but that's a load of hogwash," Pike said. He rose. "Well, I best be on my way." He went to his room and got his saddlebags and rifle.

In the hallway, Beatrice said, "I'll fix up some food you can take. Billy'll bring it to you at the stable. Don't you dare leave before he gets there."

"Yes, ma'am."

The woman lightly gripped Pike's biceps. "We owe so much to you, Mr. Pike." Before he could say anything, she placed a finger across his lips, then returned the hand to his upper arm. "Yes, we do. We are indebted to you. We can never pay it back, but like I said, you have a home here anytime you want it." She stood on tiptoes and kissed him on the cheek. Face flaming red, she smiled at him, then fled.

As Pike and Groves walked down the street, Pike glanced sideways at the marshal. "You do know, don't you, Fred, that neither Mrs. Groves nor I have designs on the other?"

"Yes, I know," Groves said with a sigh. "But it's mighty strange for a man to see his wife kiss another fella even if it is just a peck on the cheek."

"Imagine it is. I wouldn't much care for it either. But it was innocent and just a way for her to say thank you, though I don't know what for. Kind of like a sister and brother."

"You damn well know what for."

CHAPTER SIXTEEN

Pike was just finishing tightening the cinch on the sorrel when Billy Groves showed up with a burlap sack. "Ma says this should last you a few days if you're careful."

"Appreciate it, Billy."

"And Pa says to meet you near O'Connor's for a snort."

Pike and Groves had split, with the bounty hunter heading for the stables and the marshal for his office.

Pike hesitated a few moments, wondering. With his horse saddled and his saddlebags and Henry on it, he was reluctant to leave the animal.

"He'll be all right, Mr. Pike," Alf Quaid, the livery owner, said. "I'll keep an eye on him."

"Obliged."

"Can I walk with you, Mr. Pike?"

"Reckon that'd be fine. But you're not to go into the saloon."

"I won't."

"Good. Now, let's go."

As they walked down Market Street, Billy asked, "What's a snort?"

Pike chuckled. "A small glass of red-eye."

"Huh?"

"Whiskey."

"Oh. Ma says whiskey's the devil's brew. Or something like that. Says it makes a person do damn fool things."

"Best not let your mother hear you cuss like that," the bounty hunter said with another chuckle.

"I won't," Billy said, embarrassed.

"Such language is all right among men but not in front of womenfolk, and not by young boys. But it's all right here. I won't tell no one. And she's right. A snort or two, at most, is fine for a man. More than that though does make a man stupid and makes him do damn foolish things."

They spotted Groves near Walnut and Eleventh Streets and fell in step with him as they headed to Fourteenth, the marshal on Pike's left, Billy on his right.

Suddenly Pike shoved Groves, who stumbled a few feet and began reaching for his pistol, wondering why Pike had done so.

A shot rang out, then three more.

The marshal managed to yank out his pistol but the bounty hunter, far more seasoned in gunplay, was already returning fire at the two men who had fled the saloon when Pike had rescued Groves.

One of the men dropped, dead with a bullet in his chest and another in the stomach. The other turned and ran. Pike held off on firing again at the fleeing man, afraid that he might hit an innocent person.

A moment before taking off after the outlaw, Pike realized that Billy was down, and Groves was bending over him. Pike looked uncertain. Groves glanced at him and yelled, "Go!"

The bounty hunter took after the man down Walnut. The outlaw turned, racing down Sixth Street, then into an alley off that street, only to find his way blocked by a tall fence closing off the other end of the alley. He spun, firing twice with a shaking hand.

Pike stalked forward, ignoring the gunfire. He began reloading his Colt, stopping a few feet from the outlaw. "You should've just left town, boy," he said. He began firing, slowly and methodically shooting the man five times in the torso. The man slid down the wall, leaving a bloody trail behind him.

Pike walked toward the man, reloading the pistol again as he walked. As he looked down at the corpse, he reloaded his other Colt. He suddenly spun dropping to one knee, and his finger was an eyeblink from being pulled when the bounty hunter recognized Deputy Paul Malloy.

"Don't shoot, Mr. Pike," Molloy said in a shaky voice.

Pike rose. "Take care of this scum." He hurried out of the alley and toward the doctor's office. Within two blocks he saw Marshal Groves and Billy walking down Walnut Street. Relief washed over him like a refreshing rain shower on a hot summer's day.

Before he could say anything, Billy looked at him. He had old tear streaks on his cheeks and his face was pale. But he grinned. "I got shot, Mr. Pike! Ain't that something!"

"You all right?"

"Yep. It hurts like the dickens, but ain't so bad."

Pike glanced at Groves.

The marshal nodded. "Just a flesh wound, and not much of that either. He's more scared than hurt."

Pike nodded absentmindedly. "Has the rubbish been taken care of?"

"Yes. We weren't at the doc's more than a few minutes, but when we just passed there the body was gone." He paused. "The other?"

"Deputy Malloy went to fetch the undertaker."

"Good."

"Well, I best be on my way."

"Come home with me, Mr. Pike," Billy said. "You can tell Ma what happened."

"Your pa can do that better than I can, Billy."

"Please."

Pike glanced at Groves, whose blank expression gave the bounty hunter no clue as to what the marshal thought. "I don't think so, Billy."

"Oh, come on with us," Groves suddenly said, surprising Pike with a grin. "That way you can take some of the fire and brimstone Beatrice will be sendin' my way."

"Good reason for me to ride on out as fast as I can." He looked down at Billy, whose eyes pleaded with him. He didn't think this a good idea at all, but he nodded.

* * *

The door to the Groves house burst open, and Beatrice came flying out. "Billy, Billy. Are you all right?" She almost screeched as she enveloped the boy tightly in her arms.

"Let me go, Ma," Billy protested. "You're smotherin' me."

Beatrice either didn't hear the boy because she held him so tight, or she was ignoring him.

"Let him be, Beatrice. The boy's fine, though he might not be if you keep suffocatin' him."

The woman released the boy and turned venomous eyes on her husband. "How could you let him almost be killed and be so calm about it?" she demanded.

Groves sighed. "He wasn't almost killed; he just got a flesh wound. And I didn't *let* him. Two outlaws just started shootin' at us."

"It was my fault, Beatrice," Pike said quietly. "Those men were gunnin' for me. Your husband and son just happened to be with me."

Beatrice glanced from Groves to Pike and back.

The lawman nodded. "Brodie took care of it. I was too shocked to do anything," he said, shame in his voice.

"Wasn't the kind of thing you deal with regularly, Fred," Pike said. "It's more my kind of business. And I am sorry you and Billy got caught up in it. I told you I'd bring you trouble, Fred."

"You didn't bring us trouble, Brodie. Those two snakes did. Me and Billy just happened to be there when they started shootin'."

"But they were gunnin' for me."

"I know that. But the only reason they did so was because of what you did to save Beatrice and me. You hadn't done that, we'd both be dead like as not and those boys'd be runnin' free. All of 'em. But you put your life in harm's way—in danger's way—to save us. No, Brodie, you didn't cause us trouble."

Beatrice looked down at her son. "You sure you're all right?"

"Yes, Ma. Doc said it was just a scratch on my upper arm." He pointed to the bandage.

The woman turned her glance on Pike. "Once again, we are in your debt, Mr. Pike."

Pike shook his head. He was embarrassed by the praise, believing that he was the cause of trouble. It was time to get out of the lives of these good people before something more dangerous happened to them. "You don't owe me anything, Beatrice, except a good-bye." He knelt and shook Billy's hand. "You're a brave young man, Billy. And your parents are proud of you. But you better obey them."

"I will," the boy said solemnly.

"But if your ma starts scoldin' you too much, tell her to jump in the lake."

Billy's eyes widened to the size of a mule's shoe.

Beatrice gasped. Pike looked at her as he rose and winked.

It took a moment, but the woman smiled. "You are a rascal, Mr. Brodie Pike."

Pike tousled the boy's hair. "I was just joshin', Billy. You sass your mother like that, young man, and you'll have to answer to me." He shook Groves's hand and nodded at Beatrice. "I really must be goin'." When

Beatrice made a move toward him, he shook his head. "You give me another peck on the cheek, and your husband will shoot me down."

The woman looked from man to man, then grinned. "To the devil with him." Once again she gave Pike a quick peck on the cheek and, again embarrassed, fled into the house.

"Yep, you best be goin'," Groves growled. Then he laughed.

"I'll repeat what Beatrice said earlier this mornin'. You'll always have a place here, Brodie. Be safe in your travels."

Pike nodded, turned, and moved off.

When he got to the place where he had left the mule outside town, the animal was gone, as were the supplies the mule had been carrying until Pike unloaded them at this spot.

"Well," he muttered, "you'll make do." He was not too concerned. He had the sack of food from Beatrice Groves, plus a small coffeepot, mug, and frying pan in his saddlebags. He had been on the trail with less.

* * *

As he rode west toward Golden, Pike realized that any trail he might pick up of Ben Sykes and his gang that he could find would be so cold as to be considered frozen. He decided he would have to wait 'til he got some more recent information as to the outlaw's latest atrocity to take up the trail again.

He pulled into Golden midmorning the next day. He found a room, cleaned himself up and strolled over to the town marshal's office. A young, skinny deputy who appeared to be tall though he was sitting, looked up and nodded, a question in his eyes.

"I'm lookin' to see if any outlaws have caused any trouble in these parts lately."

"There's always some outlaws causin' trouble. You lookin' for bounty money?"

"Yep."

"Can't say as there's any that pay well right now, but a stack of handbills there on the corner of the desk. Take a look and choose whatever ones you want."

"You're a lot more easygoing about this than many a lawman," Pike said.

"Right now, we're missin' a couple of deputies, so it's just me and Marshal Sullivan, and the two of us have enough to do without ridin' around chasin' fellas raisin' a ruckus."

"Glad to help," the bounty hunter said with a chuckle. He looked through the papers and picked out two. "You're right, these are small-fry, but a hundred dollars is a hundred dollars. I just hope I can run 'em down soon. The longer it takes, the less profitable it becomes."

"That's the truth. Good luck in your huntin'."

"Thanks." Pike left. He decided to treat himself a little. He was not low on funds, so he had taken on these two low-reward bounties more because he needed something to do rather than because he needed the money. He thought he was due some relaxation after the gun battles and worry he had gone through in Denver. So he had a bath, shave, and haircut. He bought new clothes, including a hat to replace the bullet-punctured one. A couple of good meals, a couple hours in an almost-top-of-the-line bordello and a couple more hours in a halfway decent saloon served to take the edge off his anger at himself for having caused the Groves family so much trouble. And in the morning, when he left Golden, heading northeast, he was much refreshed.

It took less than two weeks to run down Roger Norton, and when he brought the outlaw into Golden to collect the reward, he learned that the Sykes gang had robbed a bank in Black Hawk just after Pike had left Golden on his hunt for Norton.

CHAPTER SEVENTEEN

* * *

"Hallo, the house," Brodie Pike called, stopping a few yards from the steps leading to the porch of a small, trim ranch house. He got no response, so called out again.

Moments later, a woman opened the door, holding a shotgun in her hands. Though she was small and thin, the cast of her eyes and the way she held the weapon indicated to Pike that she knew how to use it. Beyond that, she seemed to be perfectly willing to do so.

"What d'you want?"

"I was hopin' I could water my horse at your trough, and maybe get a bit of hay——or, better, grain if you have it. I'm willing to pay." He smiled, hoping to put her at ease a little. "Long as it ain't too dear."

The woman stood, the scattergun not wavering, though it was still not pointed directly at him.

"I'm willing to go set under that tree over there,"

aimin' a thumb at a cottonwood maybe fifty yards away, "till your husband gets back."

"Got no husband," she said, her voice containing equal measures sadness and determination.

"You runnin' this place all by yourself?"

"I am." It was said proudly. "Well, plannin' to."

"Hard to believe, ma'am."

"Why? 'Cause I'm a woman?"

"I gotta admit that's part of it. But not all." When she cast a questioning glance at him, he added, "I don't know as if a man could run a ranch, even a small one, without help."

"I got help," she said defiantly.

"I believe that's a large pile of claptrap." His smile faded when she began to raise the shotgun. "You don't want to do that, ma'am. It'll make one of us dead and the other mighty sad."

She looked uncertain but lowered the double-barrel a bit. "I think you best be on your way, Mister, whoever you are."

"Name's Brodie Pike. Mind if I at least water my horse? He could sure use it. You can stand there with your scattergun and keep an eye on me."

"Go on, then," she said after a moment's hesitation. She found herself becoming less fearful of this man, but she worried that it was perhaps because he was handsome and easygoing. She didn't want to fall into a trap of trusting a man who might be a bad man just because he seemed nice.

"Obliged." Pike dismounted and led the horse to the trough near the well. He loosened the animal's saddle and let it drink. He walked to the well, grabbed the ladle and filled it from the bucket sitting on top. He drank gladly, then repeated it.

As he worked, he looked over at the woman, who had moved a little closer, but still far enough away to have a good shot at him. "What happened to your husband, ma'am?" he asked.

"Killed. By some gun-totin' scum. Maybe like you."

"It's true I'm totin' guns. But I'm not scum, ma'am. I'm a good guy." He paused. "Were you molested?"

"I was away visitin' my neighbor Annie. When I got back here, Luke was dying. He lingered long enough to tell me what happened."

"He tell you what the killers looked like?"

"Not much. Medium size, three of 'em. Hard looking. Said one of 'em had a scar 'round his neck, like someone had tried to hang him."

Pike nodded. "Ben Sykes, Mike Shaw, and Dave Griffin. I've been trailing 'em for weeks. When did it happen?"

"A week——no, eight days——ago."

Pike nodded and started to tighten his saddle. "I'll be on my way then, ma'am. How much I owe you for the water?"

"You hungry?" she suddenly asked, surprising herself more than him.

"Feller like me who lives on the trail so often is always hungry, at least for good home cooking. But I need to get on their trail if they've been gone that long."

"Taking time for a meal won't delay you that much." She was still baffled at herself. She instinctively trusted this man, and while she was not attracted to him, she could use some company, a man's presence for just a little bit. It would offer her a little reassurance, she thought.

"You sure, ma'am?"

"Yes. And my name's Maggie."

"Obliged." He smiled again.

She returned it. "Go on and put your horse in the barn and let him feed. There ain't much grain but there's some corn and maybe a few oats in a barrel next to the door."

"Thank you, ma'am...I mean Maggie."

In the barn, he unsaddled the gelding, spread out some hay and topped it off with several carrots and an apple he found lying in a corner. He went straight to the trough then, tossed his hat aside and dunked his head in the tepid water. He came up shaking the water from his longish black hair.

"There's soap and a basin here on the porch," Maggie called.

Pike grinned, walked over, and made use of it. He followed Maggie inside aware of her nervousness at being alone with him. He put his hat on a peg next to the door and took a seat at the table.

"I hope this is all right," Maggie said, spooning up some kind of stew into a bowl in front of him.

"Maggie, if you were to serve me sawdust with gravy, it'd be better than anything I've eaten in the past two months."

Maggie giggled a little. "Well, I do think I'm a good cook, and if I did serve you sawdust, it'd be good tastin'."

Both laughed.

"It's a stew with some good beef we..." she choked back a sudden sob "...butchered just before..."

Pike didn't know what to say, so he said nothing, just dug into his food. After a few minutes, she regained her composure. She ignored her own bowl of stew but sipped at her coffee, managing to almost stifle her sniffles.

"I'm sorry," Maggie finally said. "I don't know..."

"It's all right, Maggie. You just lost your husband recently. And in a bad way. I've lost a loved one, too, so I know how it hurts. That hurt might never fully go away but it'll lessen over time."

"Your wife?"

He sucked in a breath then fought to compose himself as a vision of Little Raven flashed across his mind. He forced a smile onto his face. "Good Lord, no," he lied. "Ain't' a woman in the world'd be such a fool as to marry me. No, ma'am. Any woman who even gave a passin' thought to marryin' me should be locked up in an asylum for people who'd lost their reason."

"Oh, I don't know, Mr. Pike. I don't know you, of course, but I'd guess that any woman in her right mind'd find you a rather fine catch."

"Well, after feedin' me, I'd hate to insult you, Maggie, but now I do think you've lost your sense." He managed another smile.

She smiled wanly and was silent for a bit. Then she asked, "Was the food all right?"

"Well," he said, managing the hint of a mischievous grin, "I wouldn't exactly say it was 'all right,' you understand. But if you have enough left, I'd go for another heapin' bowl full."

"Of course," Maggie said with a flush of pleasure. As she was ladling more stew into Pike's bowl, she suddenly exclaimed, "Oh, dear, maybe I *am* losin' my mind!" At Pike's questioning look, she said, "The biscuits. I forgot the biscuits. I'm sorry."

"No need to be sorry. I was enjoyin' this without biscuits, but now that you remembered 'em, bring 'em on over here."

She managed a giggle and a moment later a plate of biscuits and a small bowl of butter were sitting in front of her guest, who partook of them with gusto.

Finally, Pike sat back with a satisfied sigh. "That was a fine, fine meal, Maggie." A few minutes later, Pike finished his coffee. "Well, Maggie, I best be on my way."

"Do you really have to leave already?"

"Yes'm. I got a lot of miles to put behind me and the day ain't getting longer." He rose and put on his hat. "You'll be all right here alone?"

"Reckon so. Ain't got much choice."

"I know you ain't had much time, but have you thought of sellin' the place?"

"You wantin' to buy?" It was said harshly, angrily, and not with any eagerness.

"Me?" Pike snorted. "Such a thing ain't in my blood. No, ma'am. I want nothin' to do with such a life. I just wondered if you give it some thought. Might be the best thing you could do."

"Reckon not."

"Anyone you can get to help you? Brother? Cousin? Some other kin?"

"Maybe. I'll have to think on it."

"Do so. And keep that scattergun close to hand."

"I most certainly will."

Ten minutes later, he rode out, starting in a semi-circle at the edge of the pasture behind the house. It didn't take long to pick up the outlaws' trail heading for the mountains that started to rise not far beyond the valley where Maggie planned to run her small ranch.

He pushed fairly hard. The men had more than a week's head start, and he wanted to close the gap if he could. Late in the afternoon two days later, he found an old camp amid a batch of boulders that had long ago tumbled down from the craggy slope. From the detritus, Pike figured they had spent three days here. Since it was late in the day, he decided he'd also stay the night here. He "dined" on jerky, the last of the biscuits Maggie had given him, stale now, and coffee.

Breakfast was more of the same, minus the stale biscuits. He tossed the last dregs of coffee from the pot over the fire, saddled and bridled his horse, and rode on. The track was fairly easy to follow, at least for a while. As he wound deeper into the mountain, the land grew rockier. Over the next two days, Pike lost the trail more than once and had to spend time searching for it. He invariably found it again, though at the cost of valuable hours.

The next day, just before dusk, he found another site at which he thought the outlaws had spent more than one night. Pike camped there and in the morning picked up the trail. He lost it again within an hour and spent much of the day searching for it. He finally picked it up in the afternoon, in a different place than he would have expected, and it had him wondering what the outlaws were up to.

Still somewhat surprised and confused, he began following the trail in the morning, realizing soon after that the trail was heading downward. About midmorning, he stopped, staring at the clear trail that the outlaws had left.

"Damn!" he suddenly spat. He slapped the horse's rump with the sharp ends of the reins, and the animal bolted forward.

CHAPTER EIGHTEEN

Pike yanked hard on the reins and was off his horse before it had even fully stopped. As he hit the porch running, a shotgun blast boomed from inside the house. Heedless of the danger, he charged inside, pistol in hand, and took in the scene in an instant.

One man lay on the floor a few feet from Maggie, his guts blown apart. Another man had the shotgun barrel in his hands and was wrestling Maggie for it. A third man was standing a little to the right, revolver out, ready to fire if his friend gave him a clear shot at the woman.

Pike shot him first. The man had started to turn his head toward the door, surprised at Pike's sudden entry. Pike shot him in the left eye.

The man wrestling over the shotgun with Maggie finally jerked it free and turned, wondering why his friend had fired. He had but a moment for the scene to register before his head burst from a bullet from Pike's .44.

Maggie, ashen faced at the carnage, stood for a few moments, then ran to Pike. He managed to slide his pistol away before she banged into him and squeezed him tight.

Flustered, Pike put his arms around the woman, holding her gingerly. She was shaking and sobbing. They stayed that way for several minutes before Pike gently pushed her away. "That's enough, Maggie," he said quietly. "There's work to be done here."

* * *

They rode into Middle Boulder, which he learned was now called Nederland, late that afternoon, Maggie handling the small farm wagon and Pike riding his gelding beside it. They pulled to a stop in front of a decrepit stone building between a barber shop and a saloon. It had a poorly hand-painted sign that labeled it as the marshal's office.

Before the bounty hunter could dismount, a stout man of medium height ambled up. "Maggie," he said with a tip of the hat. He looked at Pike. "And who're you, Mister?"

"President Grant," Pike replied. "Who're you?"

"I'm Marshal Emil Hastings." He did not seem pleased with the bounty hunter's response. "Now, who are you?"

"Name's Brodie Pike."

"Where's Luke?" His question was directed at the woman, but his eyes were on the bounty hunter.

Maggie started crying. "He was killed little more than a week ago."

"Why didn't you come to tell me?" The lawman's gaze snapped back to her.

"Didn't have time to. I'd been visiting Annie Mitchell. When I got back, I found Luke. I buried him and had to make sure the cattle were all right. I was plannin' to do so soon. I'm sorry, Emil."

"No need to be, Maggie. I wish I'd known, though. I would've gone after the bast...fellas who did it."

"I know." Her voice was barely a whisper.

"So what're you doing here with this fella?" the lawman asked.

"Brought in some bodies," the woman answered in a strangled voice.

The lawman's eyes raised in surprise, and he walked to the side of the wagon and looked in. "What's this all about, Maggie?" he demanded.

"These men...they...tried..." She choked back tears of fear.

"These men tried molestin' Maggie. I come along and stopped 'em."

"How'd you manage that?" the lawman asked skeptically.

"Wagged my finger at 'em and they just fell over, dead." Pike said sarcastically.

"I don't like fellas who don't answer my questions without makin' light of 'em."

"Then don't ask stupid questions." Pike watched the lawman stew for a few moments.

"I mean how'd you come to be spending time at Maggie's?"

"I wasn't spendin' time with Maggie other than to water my horse at the trough on her property the other day. Then I left. I've been chasin' these scum for weeks now and tracked 'em up into the hills. I realized soon after that they were heading back to Maggie's and I raised dust getting back there. Wasn't a minute too soon neither."

"Sounds suspicious to me," the lawman said.

"Don't care how it sounds to you." He stared at Hastings, then said, "These are the boys who killed Mr.... Heck, I don't even know Maggie's last name."

"It's Donovan," Maggie interjected.

"You sure of that, Pike?"

"Yep. What'll we do with these?" Pike chucked a thumb over his shoulder at the wagon.

"Take 'em down to Rupert's. He's the coffin maker when we need it and is the closest thing we have to an undertaker." He pointed. "Three blocks up Bridge here and around the corner of Second Street. Three places east."

Pike nodded. Before he could move off, the lawman said, "And soon as you drop 'em off, you come back and see me in my office."

"I intend to. Like I said, I've been chasin' these scum for weeks and I aim to collect the reward for 'em soon's I can."

"You can't tell me..."

The bounty hunter glared at him. "Yes, I can. And the quicker I get my money, the sooner I'll be gone." He turned his horse. "Come on, Maggie."

"You need anything, Maggie, you come see me, you hear?"

Though she was riding away, she nodded, and shouted, "I will."

As they rode along, Pike asked, "Do you have a history with the marshal, Maggie?"

"He courted me the same time Luke did. Luke won me over."

"He been troublesome to you since?"

"No, not really. He wasn't happy, of course, but he and Luke were friends. He still cares for me, I'm sure, but he's never done anything unseemly."

"He didn't seem too friendly toward me, even though I helped you."

Maggie shrugged, her face still shrouded in sadness. "I reckon he sees you as a rival, especially now that he knows Luke's dead." She choked back a sob.

Rupert, the coffin maker/undertaker, was quite happy with the largess that was delivered. "I'll take care of the wagon after I tend to these fellas," he said, "if you need to go on and do something."

"Obliged," Pike said. He looked at Maggie. "Walk or ride behind me?"

"Walk, I think. People might talk otherwise."

Pike nodded. Towing his horse behind him, he and Maggie headed down the street to the livery stable. Then it was off to get rooms, the choice if which was limited, and finally a stop at the marshal's office. The inside was no more resplendent than the rough-hewn exterior.

"You don't need to be here, Maggie," the lawman said.

Fighting back more tears, she plunked herself down in a chair. "Maybe I do."

Hastings didn't look happy but said nothing as

Pike took another chair. The marshal sat at a table that looked as if it could hold little more than a few pieces of paper before collapsing. "So, tell me again how you came to spend time with Maggie, Mr. Pike."

"I'll tell you this just this once more. You question my integrity or Maggie's virtue again and you'll regret it, even if you are wearin' a badge. Like I said, I've been trackin' these scum for weeks. Along the way, I came upon Maggie's. I watered my horse and she offered me a meal, durin' which she told me about her husband."

"And he didn't molest you, Maggie?" Hastings asked skeptically. He jumped a little as Pike kicked the table, scattering papers and such over his lap. The marshal went for his pistol.

Pike was faster, and had his Colt cocked and pointed at the lawman's head. "I told you what would happen if you questioned Maggie's modesty again. You have a choice. Put your gun away and offer Maggie a heartfelt apology…"

"Or?"

"Or get shot. Of course, I might decide to not hit something vital but it'll still be painful and put you out of commission for a while."

Hastings hesitated only a moment, then took his hand off his revolver. He looked at the woman. "I'm sorry, Maggie, I…You know how I feel about you, and when another man…"

"It's all right, Emil. Mr. Pike has shown himself to be an honorable man in the very little time I've known him, and I think you shouldn't think ill of him when there is no reason at all to do so."

The lawman looked over at Pike. "My apologies, Mr. Pike. I'm fond of Maggie and…"

"I know. She told me. As I was saying, I stumbled on Maggie's and watered my horse. She was kind enough to offer me a meal, which was mighty good after weeks on the trail. Then I left. Sykes—Ben Sykes was the leader of this bunch—and his men had headed up into the hills and I followed. I was getting close to catchin' 'em when I realized they had back-tracked and were heading for Maggie's. I got myself there just in time."

"And killed 'em all?" the marshal asked, his face blank.

"Yep," answered with a straight face.

"Rupert says one of them was killed with a shotgun blast." He paused. "And I haven't seen you carrying a scattergun."

"Rupert must be mistaken."

Hastings glanced from Pike to Maggie and back again. The faintest hint of a smile touched his lips for just a moment. He nodded. "I thought that was the case." He shifted his gaze back to Maggie. "You have a place to stay in town?"

"I have a room at Miles and Baker's hotel."

"You have the money for that?" Hastings asked, surprised.

"Mr. Pike paid for a room."

When Pike saw the lawman's jaw clench, he said, "I have a room at Mr. and Mrs. Wellington's boarding house. If you feel unease at me having paid for Maggie's room, you can certainly reimburse me."

The marshal nodded.

"And like I said, I'll be leavin' Nederland as soon as I get the reward money."

"A voucher for it should be here tomorrow or the day after."

"In my name?" A slight touch of harshness crept into his voice.

"I may be a lot of things, Mr. Pike," Hastings said angrily, "but a thief ain't one of them. I didn't earn those rewards, so I made no claim to them."

"My turn to apologize, Marshal. I've met too many lawmen who weren't so trustworthy."

The lawman grunted an acknowledgment. "May I take you to dinner, Maggie?"

The woman hesitated and glanced at Pike.

"I have some things to do," the bounty hunter said. He rose. "Let me know when the voucher arrives, Marshal," he said and headed for the door.

Two days later, Pike cashed the voucher at the local bank, a surprisingly grand brick building despite the size of the town. He bought a mule to replace the one he had lost along the trail a while back, and supplies, and loaded it all up and rode out of Nederland. He did not know where he was going or what he would do. He just knew it would be better for him, Hastings, and Maggie if he was no longer around.

CHAPTER NINETEEN

Pike sat around his lonely fire one night and thought about Maggie Donovan. It had been more than seven months since he had left Nederland and he hadn't thought of her in a while. She had been on his mind for some time after he left, but in the business of man hunting, she had faded. Until now. He didn't know what had suddenly brought her to mind, but he decided he might mosey on up to the Nederland area and check on her. After he brought in Harp Miller. The outlaw was worth a hundred dollars, a good sum for a man considered not very dangerous, but Pike had had nothing to do when he had turned over some outlaws in Golden, so he had hit the trail again.

Miller was not difficult to run down. Pike found the outlaw in a saloon in Winchester. He walked up, tapped Miller on the shoulder and said simply, "Come with me."

"And why should I do that?" the outlaw asked with bravado.

"You'll be one hurtin' fella if you don't."

Miller looked Pike in the eye and didn't like what he saw. He nodded.

Miller was no trouble on the ride to Golden. The bounty hunter collected his money and set his sights north toward Nederland. As he rode, he tried to decide how to go about approaching her. He could just ride up to the house. But if she had remarried, it might be an awkward situation, more so for her than him. He finally decided he would ride into Nederland and talk to Marshal Emil Hastings. That, too, might he awkward but less so than an unexpected visit to Maggie at her house. Unless, of course, she had married Hastings. That could really get awkward, he thought with a chuckle.

Pike rode into town and stopped at the marshal's office, but it was closed. That wasn't surprising; a lawman likely would be patrolling the town at this time of day. He stabled his horse, got a room at Miles and Baker's hotel, which was a little more reputable looking than the last time he was here and Maggie had stayed in it, and had something to eat. Then he checked the marshal's office again. The door was unlocked, and he walked in, surprised to see someone other than Hastings behind the rickety table. "Marshal Hastings around?" he asked.

"He ain't marshal no more. I am. What do you want?"

"A little courtesy would be a good start."

"Get the hell out of my office, boy."

"Or?"

"Or I'll either shoot you or chain you to the stump in back." He offered an oily grin. "Or both."

Pike laughed, surprising the lawman.

"You don't think I could?" the marshal asked in annoyance.

"Nope. Don't matter, though. You know where Hastings is?"

"Nope. Don't care neither. Now get out of my office, I got business to take care of."

Pike snorted in derision. "Business? Hell, you ain't even competent enough to wipe your ass on your own." Pike was laughing as he left, though he was alert to any possible sound of a pistol being cocked. It did not come, much to his relief. He also stayed more alert than usual in his little time outside in the town. He stuck mostly to his room for the rest of the day. After breakfast the next morning, he saddled and bridled his horse and rode out of Nederland.

Two hours later, he was in the hills a little way up from Maggie's place watching. Nothing seemed out of place, but something didn't feel right to him, though he could not place it. He rode down and around, coming up toward the front of the house as he had the first time. He was wary and even had to admit to himself more than a little concerned that he could be a target. The house looked rather unkempt, unlike it was when he had first shown up. The yard was not well cared for either. He took a deep breath and called out to the house.

A man he didn't know came out. "What do you want?" he snarled.

Pike was quickly growing tired of rude and fractious men. But he decided not to push back just yet. "I was lookin' for Maggie. I'm an old friend. I was driftin' by and thought I'd stop and say hello."

"I'm her husband, and she don't need some saddle tramp comin' by to bother her."

"I'd like to hear that from her."

The man glared a minute, then called, "Get out here, woman. Now!"

Pike was shocked when a meek-looking Maggie Donovan stepped out of the house but he did not let it show.

"Do you know this fella?"

"I met him once." Maggie's voice was soft, frightened.

"Well, tell him that I'm your husband and that you don't need some other man comin' here sniffin' around you."

"You best leave," the woman said in that small voice that shocked Pike anew.

The bounty hunter stared at her for a moment, then nodded. He touched the brim of his hat, turned his horse, and rode slowly away, a deep sense of wonder—and dread—growing in him.

It seemed evident to him that Maggie had not married for love, or even convenience. And the man who claimed to be her husband did not strike Pike as an honorable fellow. He couldn't help but wonder what had happened to Emil Hastings. The marshal obviously cared deeply for Maggie. Why she had not married him was perhaps the strangest thing about this.

He figured he should ride on; this was none of his

concern really. But he couldn't just let it rest. Despite hardly knowing her, he liked Maggie Donovan and he thought Hastings was a decent man. He had to know what was going on.

He pulled up amid the lodgepole pines outside the town and made a small camp for himself. Soon after, he was sitting with his back against a tree trunk and a cup of coffee in his hand, surveying the town. There was not much to see from here, just people the size of ants moseying or scurrying about on foot or horse-back. The town was a ragged collection of two mostly wood buildings, each bordering a wide street. Build-ings—homes, Pike guessed—were scattered around the fringes. The Caribou mill was off to his left.

He was still uncertain what to do. She was a stranger to him, really, so he had little reason to worry about her. But she had impressed him with her courage and stout heart. So he could not just ride away from the situation until he found out what was going on. If she had indeed married that unpleasant fellow and was happy about it, he would ride on. But he was certain, judging by the meekness she had not shown Pike previously, that such was not the case. So he could not let this go; he had to learn what the truth was.

Trouble was, he didn't really know how to go about it without causing a fuss that might lead to Maggie being harmed. He decided he needed to find Emil Hastings. If anyone knew what was going on, it would be the former marshal. But where to look? He had no idea where the "retired" lawman lived or of which saloons he favored. Indeed, Pike knew nothing at all of Hastings. He spent two days in his little camp, trying to decide what he would do, then he made up his mind.

He packed up his few things and rode down to the town. He stopped at McMasters's mercantile and tied the sorrel to the hitching rail outside and entered the building, which was chockablock full with anything a person could need. He was impressed at the array of goods found here in this small, still rather primitive town.

Pike waited until the two clerks served a few female customers, then stepped up to the counter.

"What can I do for you?" one clerk asked.

"You know where I might find Marshal—er, former Marshal—Hastings?"

"That rummy?" the clerk snorted. "What do you want to see that old drunkard about?"

"Drunk, eh? Well, I'm an old friend passin' through, and I thought I'd pay him a visit. Reckon I won't bother now that I know he's a sot. Well, then, I'll just get a few things and ride on out. No need to loiter just to see some snoot-faced fella."

"It's best not to see an old friend in such a condition," the clerk offered. "Better to remember 'em from better days."

"Reckon you're right. Well, I'll take a couple pounds of bacon, Arbuckle's, couple airtights of peaches, some lucifers."

Five minutes later, he walked out and hung the burlap sack of goods from his saddle horn and rode slowly away. A mile or so outside Nederland, he circled up and around on the hillside to his old camp.

As he had figured, no one had disturbed the cooking utensils he had left lying about. He hung the burlap sack from a tree, rode over the hill, and took a position behind a pine a few yards from the stream. He waited patiently and was rewarded two hours later when a small deer stopped at the stream to drink. Moments later, the animal was dead, a bullet from Pike's old Henry rifle through its skull.

Pike swiftly butchered out enough meat to last a day or two—any longer and it would go bad in the warmth even this high up—and had some hanging over the fire. A pot of coffee was heating up too. As he waited for his meal, Pike unsaddled and tended the gelding, then plopped down next to the fire. The bounty hunter ate without much enthusiasm though it had been a while since he had a meal of venison and was glad to have it.

* * *

After three nights of surreptitiously searching the town in the dark looking for Emil Hastings, Pike was about to give up and try to think of some other way to find out what was going on with Maggie Donavan and those around her. On the fourth night, however, he managed to spot Hastings staggering around the side of a saloon toward the back. Pike followed and arrived just in time to see in the moonlight Hastings relieving himself of the vileness that his stomach suddenly did not want.

"Quite a show here, Emil," Pike said dryly.

"Go to hell on a fast horse, whoever you are," Hastings managed to gargle before spewing forth more of the evilness that had taken up residency in his stomach. "Just who are you anyway?" he gasped when the latest spasm had faded.

"A friend. Maybe. You have a horse or did you sell it to buy more nose paint?"

"Go to hell," the ex-lawman said again.

"You already told me that. Sad to say, I'm on my way, just not too soon, I hope. Now, do you have a horse?"

"Yes, dammit." Hastings had a little success in straightening up. "What's it to you?"

"You're comin' with me."

"Suppose I don't plan on doin' so?"

"Then I will shove a gag in your mouth and drag you by the hair to the stable, figure out which horse is yours, and put you on it. If you don't give me any trouble, I might even saddle it for you. If you do give me trouble, I'll knock you on the head, toss you over the horse's back, and ride out with you that way."

"You ain't able to do that."

"In your state I could do damn near anything I please to you. Now, will you come along quietly?"

"You knock me out, you'll have to drag me."

"Well, my horse'll be glad to tow you to where we're going. Now, let's go."

"Just who the hell are you any..." He stopped midsentence when his body reminded him that it still contained a much too great quantity of red-eye.

"You are one pitiful sight, Emil," Pike said, but he waited until the retching stopped. Then he shoved Hastings forward.

CHAPTER TWENTY

Pike handed the former lawman a cup of steaming coffee. Hastings just grunted and shrugged. "You look like you've been et up by a wolf and shit over a cliff, Hastings," Pike said with a small laugh.

"Piss on you, Pike." Hastings blew on the coffee and took a tentative sip.

"That's not very friendly."

"Wasn't meant to be." He took another sip of coffee. "Why'd you drag me out here? Make fun of the drunk marshal…er, former marshal?"

"There is that, yep," Pike said with a grin, which dropped after a second. "What the hell's going on, Emil?"

"I'm drinkin' too much. Now give me my horse and let me be on my way." He started to rise but plopped back down with a grunt.

"You're not going anywhere, even if you were able. Now, what's going on?"

"None of your concern, Pike."

"I'm makin' it my concern." He paused. "I reckon this involves Maggie, doesn't it?"

Hastings looked up sharply through bleary eyes. "What do you know about it?" he demanded.

"Not much, which is why I'm talkin' to you. I went by the ranch to say hello..." He stopped at the glare from the former lawman. "Just to say hello, Hastings." He grinned a little. "Wanted to see if you finally got to marry her."

"Bastard," Hastings growled, throwing the contents of his cup at the bounty hunter. "You were gonna court her if I wasn't there. Or even if I was."

"Hastings, I'm already tired of this. I have no intentions of courtin' Maggie. Or anything else. I just wanted to say hello and see if she was handlin' the ranch all right. I was thinkin' she might've sold it. Or married you and you were helpin' her run things." He was surprised at the look of disgust and loss that crossed Hastings's face.

Pike was quiet for a bit, then said, "I went by the ranch and saw her and her husband. Or some foul lookin' fella who said he was her husband. She did not look happy. She looked meek and scared. I didn't know her well, but when I last saw her, she was a feisty, strong woman."

"That she is...was."

"So what happened?"

Hastings was silent for so long that Pike began to think he would not say anything. Then the former marshal said quietly, "I was plannin' on courtin' her. Not pressurin' her at all. After all, Luke was freshly gone to his reward. I'd go out to the ranch every few days to see her and help out. After a few weeks, she was beginning to warm up to me as I'd hoped she would." He fell silent again, looking sick.

Pike gently took the cup out of Hastings's hand, refilled it, and handed it back to the ex-lawman.

Hastings nodded thanks and took a hearty swallow. Pike let him be.

"Then one day when I went out there, a number of unsavory-lookin' fellas were there. Maggie was meek lookin', like you said, very unlike her. She said one of the men was her cousin and the others were his friends come to help her with the ranch. One of the men seemed to be mighty friendly with Maggie, stayin' close to her. Not touchin' her but near enough that she knew he was within arm's reach. She was afraid of him."

"Do you know if this fella is really her cousin?"

"Best I can tell, yep."

"How'd he get here? I mean, how'd he find out Luke was dead and Maggie was alone on that ranch?"

"Found out that a friend...a man I thought was my friend...had got word to him back in Kansas. How this fella knew the cousin, I don't know. And I didn't know who the cousin was. He and eight, maybe ten men, showed up one day and asked about Maggie's ranch. I sounded 'em out, and I didn't much like them. Seemed seedy to me, but if he was really her cousin, there wasn't much I could do. They didn't cause any trouble in town, so I couldn't do anything then either. A couple days later, they were gone."

Hastings grew silent again, and Pike asked, "You think you could eat something?"

"Ain't sure. Reckon I should try, though." His expression indicated that he was nowhere near certain that eating would be a good idea.

Pike nodded and set some bacon on the fire. Then with some hesitation, he went to his saddlebags and pulled out a small bottle of whiskey. He walked over and handed it to Hastings. "Hair of the dog but only one swallow. Try to take more than that and I will beat you bloody."

Hastings nodded in resignation. He took the bottle and stared at it for a few moments. Then he tilted it up and took a healthy swallow. Finished, he eyed the rest, seeming to debate whether to try another swallow, but then decided not to. He handed the bottle back to Pike. "Thanks," he mumbled.

The bounty hunter nodded, took the bottle, and put it away. Before long, bacon was cooked, and a new pot of coffee was ready. With only one plate and one mug, they had to share, which they did without talking.

Done, the former marshal went behind a tree to take care of business, and Pike could hear him retching again. Hastings came back to the fire looking ashen.

"It'll get better," Pike said.

"If I don't die first." He paused. "Where's my Colt?"

"In my saddlebags. I didn't think you'd need it for a while."

Hastings nodded, then groaned as he regretted it.

"Maybe you should get some more sleep, Emil."

Hastings grunted but moved away from the fire and curled up under a tree. In moments he was asleep.

Pike watched the former lawman, wondering just what was going on here. Nothing was as it should be. A meek, cowardly Maggie Donovan, a usually sober marshal now a drunk without a badge. None of it made sense. Something bad—really bad—had happened.

He sighed. He thought that perhaps things would not be so bad if he had just left Maggie's ranch and kept on going in the first place. But he knew that things would not have changed if he had, except possibly for the worse. Still, he felt some responsibility, and he was determined to make it right, as right as it could be made at least.

* * *

Hastings looked almost human when he awoke and gratefully took the cup of coffee Pike handed him. "Thanks," he mumbled. After a few swallows, he said, "Made a right stupid ass of myself, didn't I?"

"You ain't the first; won't be the last."

Hastings grimaced. "I'd wager you never made an ass of yourself."

"You'd be wrong on that." When the ex-lawman looked at him in question, Pike hesitated, then said, "Just a few years ago," he said quietly, thinking back over the time with sadness, "I hit my woman. Shocked me more than it did her. I run off and got stinkin' drunk. I was heavin' my guts onto the ground when her brother showed up. Crazy Hawk had been plannin' to punish me somehow, but decided I was doing that myself. I..."

"Crazy Hawk? She was an Indian? You were married to an Indian?"

"Yep. A Ute named Little Raven." He almost smiled at the horror on Hastings's face.

"Why?… How…What…?"

"Long story that you don't need to hear."

"Well, at least you got rid of her, I'm glad to say."

Pike's expression darkened. He rose and stalked off, ignoring Hastings's muttered and regretful "Damn." A short while later, he went back to the fire.

"I'm sorry, Brodie. I…"

"Shut your trap, Emil. Just shut it."

Hastings nodded glumly.

After some moments of tense silence, Pike asked, "What happened after those fellas left town?"

"I rode out to Maggie's the next day. The cousin, Tink Conroy's his name, I found out, wouldn't let me see her. Said I wasn't kin and had no place out there. Said they'd done nothin' wrong, and I had no reason to come and pester them. Told me to hit the trail. So I did."

"Without a challenge?"

Hastings's head dropped in shame, then rose again. He looked at Pike in defiance. "I ain't a gunman like you. Oh, I can use my Colt if I have to, but I ain't a well-practiced man with it. And there were six, seven of 'em standin' 'round. Might've been more in the house for all I knew. So I skedaddled." He gave a rueful smile. "I rode slow though."

Pike nodded. "Sensible." He paused. "Do you know exactly what happened to Maggie?"

"No. But it must've been mighty bad to have crushed her spirit like it did."

"I agree. What happened after you left her place?"

"Few days later some of 'em were in town causin' a ruckus. I was tryin' to settle 'em down. Figured if I could get 'em to the judge and they were fined a little, it might cool 'em off." He paused. "Then somebody thumped me on the head and I went out. Woke up chained up in the back of my own jail." The bitterness in his voice was strong. "One of those bastards was wearin' my badge, and my Colt was on that rickety old table. Even with the headache I had, I hated the laughin' they were doin' at my expense."

"Any man would've."

"Bah. They finally let me loose with a kick in the pants to the laughter of much of the town. I skulked off to my house and got my extra Colt and was ready to head to the jail and get to shootin' when I decided I couldn't take 'em all and might need some help. Everyone I talked to, all friends, or had been friends, wanted no part of going up against them." He spit into the fire, anger flaming his face.

"Can't say as I blame 'em," Pike said quietly. "Bunch of shopkeepers and such."

Hastings sighed. "I know. Didn't think so at the time. It was hurtful that not a one of 'em said they'd try to help. Like you said, though, shopkeepers ain't about to face off against a bunch of gunmen. Conroy's men killed a few citizens they said were harassing 'em. I didn't believe 'em but there wasn't much I could do then either. That also might have had something to do with everyone refusing' to help me. Couldn't see it then, though."

"That what led up to this?" Pike asked, waving a hand up and down in Hastings's direction indicating his dishevelment.

"Yeah. After a couple weeks of being told that no one would help, I tried to drown myself with forty-rod." He sighed in despair again, then shrugged. "Whiskey became the only friend I had in Nederland," he said, face burning with shame.

"Rotgut ain't a very good friend, Emil."

"You think I don't know that, dammit, Brodie? But once I sank into that bottle, there was no way of swimmin' out."

"You got a start here."

"Ain't gonna work."

Pike stared at the former marshal and shook his head. "Think you'll be all right here for a spell?" he asked.

"Plannin' to leave me here for being such a coward, eh?"

"Nope, plannin' to go into town and get some supplies."

"What for?"

"So I don't starve when I start payin' back those devils for what they've done to Maggie."

"I thought you were just friends, acquaintances more so, with her." Anger touched his voice.

"Yep. And friends do for friends. Unlike the people of Nederland not helpin' a former lawman who was supposed to be their friend."

He left Hastings there stewing as he saddled his

horse, then led it back toward the fire. "Your saddle is sittin' next to the tree your horse is tied to. Go on back to town if you want." He tossed the half-empty whiskey bottle at Hastings, where it landed with a dusty thud in the dirt near the former marshal's knee. "Crawl back inside or toss it away and be a man, Emil. Your choice." He climbed on his horse and slowly picked his way down the hill without looking back.

CHAPTER TWENTY-ONE

A few hours later, Pike rode back into his camp holding the rope to a small mule on which were packed some boxes and bags.

Hastings stood, saying nothing.

Pike saw the whiskey bottle where it had been. From his perch on the gelding, he thought the contents looked about the same level as when he had left. He dismounted and clapped Hastings on the shoulder.

"You're a brave man, Emil Hastings. Most men who go down the whiskey trail never find their way back again."

"I ain't back yet. Not all the way."

"Got to start somewhere." He took a bag from the mule. There's some roasted chicken in there and some biscuits. Coffee beans too. Get the coffee started. Warm up the chicken if you're of a mind to while I tend to the animals."

Before long Pike was heading toward the fire. The

smell of fresh coffee and warming chicken was entic-
ing. Then he stopped. Hastings stood there with the
bottle of rotgut in his hand. Pike said nothing.

Neither did Hastings, who pulled the cork on the
bottle and dumped the whiskey out. "Hope you
weren't plannin' to have some of that yourself,
Brodie," the former lawman said, a wisp of loss in his
voice.

"Nope."

The two sat and started eating. Hastings had a
little trouble keeping the mug of coffee steady in his
shaking hand, but he managed.

"Took a lot of courage to leave that bottle where it
was while I was gone," Pike said quietly. "It took even
more to do what you just did with it."

"Seems maybe foolhardy now." Hastings paused.
"But I reckon I'm glad I did it. Might know more in
the mornin'. I'm dreadin' how I'll feel then."

"You'll do fine. And, speakin' of mornin'..." Pike
walked to where he had stacked the supplies and
grabbed a burlap sack and tossed it to his companion.

With a question in his eyes, Hastings opened it.
The questioning look changed to surprise.

Pike grinned. "Figured you'd want some new
duds," he said as Hastings pulled out a shirt and pants,
bandanna, suspenders, and socks.

"Where'd you get all this?"

"Your place. I found out where you lived and let
myself inside."

"Always knew you were a thief, Pike."

The bounty hunter's grin slipped off his face.

"Considerin' the circumstances, I'll let that pass, Hastings."

"Sorry, Brodie. It was meant mostly in jest. Most men don't like others pokin' around in their things."

Pike nodded. "You're right there. I did consider, though, takin' that ten thousand dollars you had stashed behind that cupboard." A smile touched Pike's lips.

"The what?" Hastings asked, eyes wide. "I don't have a…" Then he grinned. "Got me there, Brodie. Hell, if I had anything near ten thousand dollars, I'd be livin' the good life in Denver."

"I know. My little jest. I didn't touch anything, Emil. Just found those clothes, stuck 'em in a bag and loaded 'em on the mule."

"Well, I'm much obliged." He paused and grinned ruefully. "Reckon I could use a bath too."

"No reckonin' about it. I brought soap too."

"Think I'll wait 'til mornin'."

"I suppose I can stand the stench 'til then."

Hastings finally broke the silence that had grown around the two men. "I know you don't think much of me, Brodie, but I'd like to help you when you go against those men."

"You're not afraid?"

"Scared down to my toes."

"But you still want to help?"

"Yep."

"Likely be dangerous."

"I know that." He sighed and held Pike's gaze. "I should be all right in a couple days, once all that bug juice slithers out of my insides. If you can wait that long." The last was a question.

"Reckon a couple days won't matter none."

"I'll need my Colt back."

Pike nodded. "It's still in my saddlebags."

"You ain't afraid I'll steal that ten thousand you got stashed in there?"

Pike laughed. "As someone I know once said, "If I had anything near ten thousand dollars, I'd be livin' the good life in Denver.""

Both men laughed.

"There's gear to clean and oil in my saddlebags too. And cartridges."

Hastings soon had his revolver back in good working order—it had taken a beating in his drunken ramblings. He opened the box of cartridges. His hands were shaking so bad he kept dropping shells as he tried to stick them in the cylinder.

"Let me help," Pike said quietly, reaching out.

"No," Hastings snapped.

Pike nodded, pleased.

* * *

Cleaned and dressed in fresh clothes, his Colt holstered at his side, Hastings looked much better, and he said so, as he sat across the fire from Pike.

"Looks like you've wrestled that rotgut to the ground, Emil."

"Hope so. Feels like I got the upper hand anyhow."

They ate quietly, then sat back with another cup of coffee each.

"Do you have a plan?" Hastings asked.

"Sure. Ride on out there, grab Maggie, blow up the house and shoot all the outlaws, then ride off."

The former marshal laughed. "I think there's a few flaws in that plan, Brodie."

"I don't have a plan. Don't have enough information. I'm thinkin' I'll take a night or two to sneak around town to see if I can learn anything. If I can't, I'll head out to Maggie's and snoop around there to see what I can learn. Once I do that, hopefully I can come up with a plan that won't get Maggie—or us —killed."

"Well, that sounds like a plan. Want me to come along down there?" Hastings asked, pointing to the town below.

"I think you're a mite too shaky still. And I also have a little concern, not much mind you, that you might face too much temptation."

Hastings's face clouded with anger but quickly gave way to resignation. He nodded.

Hastings paced for most of the day, occasionally sitting. But that did not last long before he was on his feet again. Pike said nothing. He had never been in that position so he did not really know what the former lawman was going through, but he imagined it was bad. Still, there was nothing he could do.

As darkness grew, Pike saddled his horse. "You gonna be all right, Emil?" he asked.

"Yeah," Hastings growled, uncertainty touching his voice.

Pike started to speak but slapped his mouth shut. Anything he said now, he figured, would not make the situation any better. He simply rode off, once again heading down the hill toward Nederland.

* * *

Pike's arrival woke Hastings, who tumbled out of his bedroll, wiping the sleep from his eyes. "Brodie?"

"Yep." He stopped and dismounted. "Brought a guest too."

"Guest?" Hastings asked, suddenly worried.

Pike hauled a hog-tied and gagged man off the back of another horse.

The former marshal grabbed a burning brand from the fire and held it over the man. "It's one of them," he muttered, worry shifting to anger.

"Yep. I thought you might like to be around when I had a chat with him."

"Chat?"

"Since he's one of them, he might have some valuable information."

"Can I take part in this chat rather than just be around?"

"I think that would be possible, yes. Drag him closer to the fire, then tend to his horse."

Dawn was just beginning to edge its nose over the ridge as the two men sat and poured coffee. Pike tossed some bacon into the frying pan and before long he and Hastings were downing it.

By the time they finished, it was daylight, though some gray clouds were lingering over the hills. Pike rose, then knelt next to the hog-tied man and pulled the gag from his mouth.

"Water," the man croaked.

Pike nodded to Hastings who got a canteen and handed it to the bounty hunter, who poured some on the man's mouth. The man choked some but managed to swallow a little. They went through it again. Then Pike asked, "What's your name?" It was said quietly but there was no weakness in it.

The man hesitated, then said, "Seamus Coyle."

"Welcome to our humble camp, Mr. Coyle. We'll be askin' you some questions."

"I ain't answerin' anything."

"Now is not the time to talk. That will come soon enough. And I must warn you that not answering will be painful to you, even debilitating. If you live."

Coyle's eyes shifted from Pike to Hastings. "You're that drunk former marshal, the one we..."

"I am," Hastings said tightly. "But I'm sober enough to help persuade you to answer our questions. Indeed, I look forward to doing so. I might be disappointed, though, if you answer right away."

"What're you and your fellow scum doing in Nederland and vicinity?" Pike asked.

"Havin' us a little spree. Do some drinkin' and whorin', especially up at the ranch." He grinned insolently up at Hastings.

Pike went to punch Coyle, but Hastings grabbed his arm. When the bounty hunter looked at him, he said, "Allow me."

Pike hesitated only a moment before nodding.

Hastings went to the fire and plucked out a branch about two feet long and a couple inches around. He returned to Coyle's side and placed the burning end of the branch on Coyle's chest.

"Hey, what're you doin'?" Coyle squawked, his voice panicky.

"Mr. Pike asked you a question. We're waitin' for an answer. A real answer. And you might want to hurry. There's already a hole in your shirt."

"All right! All right! Move that thing!"

Hastings lifted the branch. "Answer."

"We rode into Nederland originally to check on things, like what kind of law was around." He looked askance at Hastings. "When they decided there was no threat to anything we might want to do, half the men went out to the ranch."

"Maggie's place?"

"Who? Oh, is she the woman who owned the place?"

"Owned?" Hastings asked, worry in his voice.

"She don't own it no more." He saw Hastings's look of puzzlement. "Reckon you don't know. You had 'resigned' when the others came back to town, Taylor Franks married that woman."

"Was she willin'?" Hastings was having trouble keeping his temper under control.

"Hell, I don't know. It was all legal, though. They got married by a preacher. Then they went to what passes for a land office around here and transferred the title to him."

"How'd they convince Maggie to do either of those things?" Pike asked.

"Ain't sure, but Tink—and Taylor—can be mighty

persuasive when they want. And when they have eight or ten men with 'em."

"Who are those two?"

"Tink Conroy is the woman's cousin, the leader. Like I said, Taylor married her. I think he's Tink's cousin."

Hastings's teeth were clenched, and he looked like he was ready to haul out his Colt and shoot Coyle.

Pike reached out a hand to steady him. "Not now," he said quietly. "What happened after this so-called marriage and title transfer, Coyle?"

"The ones who had come into town went back to the ranch. The rest of us stayed in town in case of trouble."

"That when you killed those people?"

"Yeah. Had our way with some of the women in town too."

"Why all this for that ranch?" Pike asked. "It ain't that big and doesn't run many cattle. Can't be worth much."

"Stage way station."

CHAPTER TWENTY-TWO

"Ah, Mr. Coyle, that's not just a pile of horse manure, that's an entire mountain of horse manure. There's no need for a stage way station out there. How about you tell us the truth."

"They'll kill me if they find out that I told."

"I might kill you if you don't. Emil, how's about you warm up Mr. Coyle's chin a bit."

Hastings started to bring the burning end of the branch toward Coyle's neck.

"Wait! Wait!" the hog-tied man screeched. He licked his lips nervously. "He plans to increase the herd, make the place a real ranch. He figures he can sell the beef to the minin' camps and in places like Boulder, maybe even Denver."

"And how does he plan on increasin' the herd? Unless he's got a heap of money or some rich backers, there ain't but one way he can do that. Rustlin'," Pike said.

"I didn't say that," Coyle said nervously.

"Didn't have to. Where's he plan on doin' this rustlin'? There ain't many ranches in these parts. And no big ones. At least not that I know of."

"If he was plannin' on rustlin', and I ain't sayin' he is, I don't know where he might do it. Maybe out on the plains, bring 'em here to fatten 'em up before sellin' 'em. He'd need a place for that. If he was to do any rustlin', that is."

Pike thought that over, then asked, "How many men are there?"

"Twelve includin' Tink, but he was expectin' four or five more. They're supposed to be bringin' some stolen cat..." He clamped his mouth shut.

"Pretty bad odds, Brodie," Hastings said. "Maybe we should..." A sharp wave of Pike's arm silenced him.

"How many are left in town?"

"Just two, no, three. Magruder was hangin' back for some reason. The rest of us were supposed to pull out this mornin' and head to the ranch. Those two would keep an eye on things. Oh, and the marshal, too, I reckon." He cast a fearful glance at Hastings.

"None of this seems right," Pike said after some moments of thought. "Unless he plans to get his hands on several hundred head of cattle somehow, he doesn't need almost twenty men. This doesn't make any sense." He paused again, then asked, "What else do you know about this, Mr. Coyle?"

"Nothing, I swear."

"This is silver country, Brodie. You know that," Hastings said.

"So?"

"Maybe the ranch is just a smoke screen. They make it look like a working ranch, maybe even add some cattle—likely by rustlin'—to build up the herd to make it look good but it's really a headquarters for those men to rob silver-carrying stages or anything else with a good supply of it."

"That sound right to you, Coyle?"

"I never heard that, but Tink and Taylor don't tell us boys much."

Pike nodded. "Anyone gonna miss you, Coyle?"

"Doubt it," Coyle said with a sour look on his face. "At least not for a while. They'll think I got drunk and passed out somewhere."

Pike sat for a few moments, then nodded. "Cut him loose, Emil."

Hastings looked at him, puzzlement written on his face. Then he shrugged, tossed the burning branch back into the fire, and knelt to cut the ropes holding Coyle.

"I imagine he would be able to do anything after being tied up like he was," Pike said. "But keep a boot on his neck."

Hastings did as he was told.

Coyle stretched out his legs. "That feels bet…" He suddenly screamed when Pike stomped on one leg, cracking both bones in Coyle's lower leg.

"Was that necessary, Brodie?" Hastings asked surprised and a little shocked.

The bounty hunter glared at him, then said, "He's one of the ones mistreatin' Maggie."

The shock was replaced by anger. "Want me to break his other leg?"

"Is that necessary, Mr. Coyle?"

"No," the man hissed in pain.

"Good. Emil, go saddle his horse."

When that was done, Pike and Hastings lifted Coyle into the saddle. The outlaw weaved a little and his face was pasty.

"I got some advice for you, boy. Ride like hell away from here. I suggest you go southeast and don't stop 'til you get to Pueblo. You go into Nederland, you'll likely find an unfriendly welcome. You go to the ranch and Tink will kill you for sure. You stop in Denver or even Boulder, they'll never believe that a bounty hunter and a marshal—they'll figure Emil's still marshal—would do something like this."

"But I got no weapon or..."

"You're lucky to be leavin' here alive, Coyle. If you'd rather, I can tie you to a tree, spread some bacon grease all over you and leave you here to be found by the nearest bear or pack of wolves."

"I'm goin'!"

Pike slapped the animal's rump and the horse darted off.

"What do we do now, Brodie? About what you think might be going on?"

"I don't give a damn if they rob every stage between here and Pueblo, Emil. I don't give a damn about 'em rustlin' cattle either. This is about saving Maggie."

Hastings nodded.

"My only concern is that the men'll be spread out, some rustlin', some robbin' the mines' bounty, some staying close to hand to watch over the cattle. And a few of 'em, including this Tink fella, are likely waiting for those other boys to show up."

"Would make it hard to take on all of 'em, wouldn't it?"

"Yep."

"So, what now?"

"We rest a bit, maybe have a little food, then ride down there." He pointed to Nederland.

"What for?"

"Cut down the odds a little." When Hastings looked at him in question, he added, "Coyle said two men were left in town. We take care of them and with Coyle out of the way, there's three less scum to worry about."

Hastings nodded. "Guess I got a lot to learn," he said with a note of sadness at his lack of skill on his face.

"If I were you, I'd forget about all this as soon as you can. No decent man should have to learn such things, and if he does, he needs to forget 'em."

"You're a decent man, Brodie."

"You don't know me well enough to say that. Hell, you don't know me at all. I've killed men in all manner of ways, many of them quite dreadful. When some men violate an eleven…" He turned and stalked off into the trees.

* * *

"I won't think less of you if you want to stay here," Pike said as he and Hastings saddled their horses.

"You need me. You don't know what these fellas look like."

"I can figure it out. Did so with Coyle."

"I meant to ask, how did you know Coyle was one of 'em?"

"Kept my ears open, listened to how people were reacting to others. Saw a few of 'em swaggerin' around town, actin' like they were runnin' the town. I could see their faces, but when they split up, I followed one of them."

"Coyle."

"Yep. Like I said, you don't have to go. You likely will be recognized if you get anywhere near a light."

"I'm going. If they see me, they'll see the old Marshal Emil Hastings, not the drunken Emil Hastings." There was worry in his voice but also determination.

"It'll lead to killin'."

Hastings turned toward Pike and rested an arm on the saddle. "I killed a man once, Brodie. It wasn't a pleasant thing, but he needed killin' and I happened to be the one to do it. I'd hoped to never do it again, even when I took the job as marshal. But these two men are part of the rabble that have violated Maggie. Like you said, that's all that matters. The rest doesn't concern us." His voice had a hitch in it. "And they deserve killin'."

"Then what?" Pike yanked the cinch tight.

"Then I stand by you and go after the rest of those animals. And I'll kill every damn one of 'em I can."

"And what after that?"

"I don't know. Depends some on Maggie, I guess.

But I don't plan on more killin'. And if that means giving up a job as lawman to become a shopkeeper or something, so be it."

"Now that's a decent man talkin'. But have you given any real thought to Maggie? Are you willin' to accept her after she's been used by a bunch of outlaws?" His voice was harsh.

"I...No, I never...I ..."

"You need to, Emil. And you need to think about what she thinks of herself after the degradation she's suffered. Will she want you, or any other man after all this?" Pike got no answer. "Let's ride."

* * *

Pike and Hastings tied their horses to a tree behind one of the few stone buildings a bit off the city center. "Got a place to start, Emil?"

"They spend a lot of time at McCorkle's saloon, or at least they did. And," he added, embarrassment creeping into his voice, "Madam Beth's."

"High-class place?"

"As high-class as it gets around here."

"These fellas can afford it?"

"Ain't likely they're payin'." He paused. "I'd rather start elsewhere." Seeing Pike's questioning look, he added, "My office."

The bounty hunter stared at him for a moment, then grinned tightly. "Looking to get your old job back, eh?"

"Something wrong with that?" the former lawman growled.

"Nope. I think it's a fine idea. But do you think he'll be there at this hour?"

"Ain't likely I suppose, but I aim to find out."

"So, let's mosey on over there and see if that son of a goat is there."

"If he ain't there, I'll find him."

"What about the other two?"

"If Hollis Magruder isn't in the office, he'll probably be with them."

"All right, Emil, let's go."

"Right. But we better go a roundabout way, keep to the shadows." He took several steps, then stopped. "To hell with that. We'll just march on down Second Street here and then Jefferson."

Pike and Hastings were surprised to find Magruder sitting on a chair behind the rickety table in his office. The pseudo marshal had a half-dressed, frightened, red-faced woman on his lap.

Magruder looked up in surprise, then grinned but that quickly faded to annoyance. "Go and get yourself another drink, Emil," he snapped. Then he grinned again. "I got important business to attend to."

Hastings ignored him, instead addressing the woman, "He molest you yet, Miz Rachel?"

She shook her head. "Just this so far. He…"

"No need to say more. Get out, girl, and do so fast."

Annoyance returned to Magruder's face. "Don't you move, woman," he commanded, tightening his grip on her.

But the woman tore herself from his grasp, grabbed her dress and fled outside.

"That was a damn rotten thin thing to do, Hastings," Magruder said in an aggrieved voice.

"My heart breaks for you. At least there's one woman in town who hasn't been molested by you and your ilk. Now, where are the others who were left in town?"

"I don't know what you're talkin' about."

"Coyle told us the main group left, leavin' behind him, you and two others."

The pseudo lawman's face clouded with anger. "I don't know anybody named Coyle. Now get lost."

Hastings eased his pistol out and then slammed the barrel across Magruder's mouth. "I reckon you'll have a heap of trouble talkin' what with a bunch of your teeth littering the table there, a mouthful of blood, and lips that are already swellin' up, but I suggest you do. Now, where are the others?"

"McCorkle's. I was gonna meet 'em there when I finished my business with…you know…we…"

"No need to spell out your revoltin' plans."

"What're you gonna do with me now?" Magruder's words were garbled but mostly understandable.

"Reckon we could chain you up in back, I reckon. Like you did me. Or kill you. What do you think, Brodie?"

"How'd you keep prisoners with no cells?"

"Well, we never had much in the way of real prisoners, mostly drunks and some fellas lettin' off a little steam. We'd chain 'em up to a big ol' loose tree trunk in the back. We could do that with this fella." He jerked a thumb at Magruder.

"Considerin' the bunch he's runnin' with and what they've done, I don't think that'd be near enough."

"So, what do you suggest?"

"Well, let me cogitate on it a spell. I reckon I can think of something appropriate for our friend here." He grinned at a bleeding, suddenly sweating Magruder.

"How much does that stump weigh, Emil?"

"I don't know. Hundred pounds or so, maybe a bit more, I reckon. Hard to tell, but it took two of us to carry it in here, though me and the other fella ain't circus strongmen. I only saw one fella move it even a little by himself, and he was a hell of a big man."

Pike grinned tightly. "I reckon it won't be as bad as he deserves, but I think I have an idea. Come on, Magruder."

"What're you gonna do?"

"You'll find out." He grabbed Magruder's hair, hauled him up, and shoved him toward the back of the small stone building.

CHAPTER TWENTY-THREE

"Got some rope, Emil?"

"Not in here. Reckon there's some on a nearby horse that we could 'borrow'."

"Doesn't sound like something a marshal would do."

Hastings grinned. "I'm not a marshal anymore, though I reckon I will be again soon enough." He headed outside.

As the former lawman left, Magruder tried to jerk free of Pike's grasp, but the bounty hunter slammed his face against the stone wall, which took the fight out of the outlaw.

When Hastings returned, Pike said, "Tie him up good and tight, Emil. Hands behind his back, legs out." As the former marshal worked, Pike clasped the manacle held to the stump by a chain held by two large spikes around Magruder's left ankle. Then he pulled the bandanna off Magruder's neck and stuffed it deep into the outlaw's mouth.

Hastings stood and grabbed the marshal's star from Magruder's shirt.

"Come on and give me a hand, Emil," Pike said.

"With what?" Hastings was puzzled.

"Put this stump on top of Magruder so he doesn't go anywhere."

Hastings's bafflement changed to concern and doubt. "You sure that's a good idea?" he asked.

Pike stared at him for a few moments, then jerked his head toward the front of the building. "Go on outside."

"But…"

"Go on, get."

When Hastings was walking tentatively toward the front, Pike knelt and tested the weight of the stump. "Well, ol' Brodie, let's see just how strong you are." He grabbed the stump and lifted, straining, his legs wobbling a little with the effort, but he finally managed to settle it on Magruder's chest. He fell back on his rump, breathing heavily. "Damn thing weighs more than a hundred pounds," he muttered.

After a couple of minutes, Pike rose a bit unsteadily. He stood for some moments, letting his muscles recover. Then he looked down at Magruder, who was struggling to breathe with his mouth closed off and the weighty log on his chest.

"You threw in with the wrong boys, Magruder. And now you're payin' for your foolishness. Goodbye."

The outlaw's eyes bulged as he vainly tried to scream.

Pike grinned and walked outside. He found Hastings standing with his back on the stone building.

"I'm sorry, Brodie."

"For what?"

"Not helpin'."

Pike shrugged. "Don't concern yourself, Emil. I did what had to be done. Ain't the first time, and likely won't be the last."

"But..."

"Look, Emil," Pike said, taking in the sickly look on Hastings's face, "some men can do such things, some can't. Like I said before, you're a decent man, and decent men don't do such things. I should've never asked you to help. I should've just sent you out here without tellin' you what I was plannin'."

"Like hell. You're helping me. And Maggie. I should be able to do what needs doing."

"Torturin' a man—and that's what this is I reckon —doesn't set well with some fellas. No shame in that. I've done a lot worse in my days. More times than I care to remember." He stared into the night and continued, almost as if he were talking to himself. "I never regretted any of the things I've done, since all the men I handled in such harsh ways deserved it. However, it seems like it too often comes back to me, injurin' people I tried to help." He sighed. "And while I don't regret any of it, I figure that when my time comes to depart this earth, I doubt Saint Peter will be waitin' at the pearly gates ready to offer me a friendly greetin'. Ol' Beelzebub, on the other hand, well, he'll be waitin', and I reckon his reception will be mighty warm." He smiled ruefully.

"I don't think…"

"Let's go find those other boys," Pike said gruffly, stepping off into the darkness.

Ten minutes later they were standing on each side of the open doorway of McCorkle's saloon. "You were right, Emil," Pike said. "Saves us from huntin' through the town for 'em."

"So what do we do?"

"Go in and invite them to leave Franks's employ. Permanently."

"You'd just go and shoot 'em down where they stand?"

"Yep."

"Who gave you the right to make that judgment?"

Pike looked at him with cold, hard eyes. "I gave me that right. The moment those men abused Maggie, stole her ranch, and began to bully the folks here—includin' humiliatin' you—they lost any right to being treated in a civil manner."

"But how do you know that…"

"It doesn't matter that they might not've been at the ranch when Franks took it over. Nor do they have to be the ones who killed those townsfolk. They're part of Franks's gang and don't deserve any consideration." He saw the indecisiveness in Hastings's stance and grabbed the former lawman by the shoulder and dragged him away from the light spilling out of the saloon. "You have to make up your mind, Emil. Here and now. Are you with me or not?"

When Hastings hesitated, Pike snapped. "Get out of here, Emil. Go home, go wander the mountains, go crawl back into the bottle. I don't care. Just get out of my way."

"But I..."

"There's no buts, boy. I can't rely on a man who's indecisive. I need a partner who won't hesitate even an instant in doing what needs doing. That'll get both of us killed and won't do a damn thing to help Maggie. These men are evil. That's all you need to know. They will not hesitate even a heartbeat to kill you. If you hesitate even that heartbeat, you'll be dead." He paused and clapped a hand on Hastings's shoulder. "I said it before, Emil, you're a decent man, and decent men generally ain't called upon to do what needs doing here. There's no shame in ridin' off. This ain't your kind of business. Just go off somewhere and think about whether you want to take care of Maggie after what she's been through."

"You can't face all those men alone," Hastings said, aghast.

"I've faced worse odds and worse men. I'll be fine, but you gotta go. I can't be worryin' about whether you'll back my play or hesitate at the wrong moment. That could be fatal to me, and I ain't hankerin' to go to my reward just yet."

"I..." The ex-lawman shut his trap. With head hanging, he began to shuffle off, but stopped at Pike's words, though he did not turn.

"You'd be best if you don't go back down the whiskey trail. Maggie'll need you. And if she wants to get her old life back, she'll want—no, need—a decent man, not a drunk. Or some hard-edged man hunter."

Hastings began shuffling off again. Pike watched

for a few moments, hoping that Hastings would find himself. Then he turned and headed back to the saloon door; he could not afford to worry about Emil Hastings now.

Pike rested one hand on a batwing door in preparation of opening it as he drew a Colt. Then he left the revolver where it was. He shook his head in annoyance. While he was generally not a man inclined to shoot others, even outlaws, in the back, he was not one to do so with impunity either. But in deference to Hastings's concerns, he decided to give these two a chance, as risky as that might be. He pushed past the doors into the saloon.

It was an unprepossessing place with few small tables scattered around the log building. A real, though small, bar was off to one side and behind that was a short plank resting on two barrels holding a selection of whiskey bottles that the bounty hunter figured were all filled with the same rotgut. The two men Pike wanted were standing at the bar, and about ten men were sitting at the tables. Everyone looked at Pike when he entered. He scanned the room quickly and decided there was no danger from anyone but the two outlaws. He strolled over to the bar, and many of the patrons began inching toward the door.

Pike ordered a whiskey. When it was placed on the bar in front of him, he turned to the men and asked, "How about I buy you boys a drink?"

The two looked at him and laughed. "Now why in hell would you buy us a drink, Mister?" the one with a blue shirt countered.

"Maybe he thinks we'll let him join our organization if he buys us a drink," the other one, wearing a green shirt, said.

"Nah. He might be wearin' that fancy gun rig, but I reckon he's scared and is hopin' that if he buys us a drink or two that we'll not bother him. So, what is it, Mister?"

"*Your* organization?" Pike said with a chuckle. "You couldn't organize a poker game between you and your mutton-headed pal there." He grinned insolently.

"Now, we've been real friendly so far," Blue Shirt said, "but we're losin' patience. Now go on your way like a good little boy. We don't need to be takin' drinks from the likes of you."

"Why'd you offer to do that anyway?" Green Shirt asked.

"Wanted you to have a farewell drink on me."

"Farewell?" Blue Shirt asked, looking at his companion in question.

"Yep. You see, you have two choices. You either drop those gun belts and ride on out of Nederland in any direction but toward the ranch."

"What ranch?" Green Shirt asked with a snort.

Pike cast a gimlet eye on him.

"Well, us moseyin' on because the likes of you is askin' ain't likely, but I was wonderin', what's our other choice." Blue Shirt was trying to hold in his laughter.

"You die, here and now."

The two outlaws could no longer constrain laughter.

"We're gonna die?" Blue Shirt said around guffaws. "Here and now?"

"It's what I said, boys, and it's what I meant." His face hardened. "Now, since you boys don't feel the need for a last drink, make your choice."

"You insufferable son of a bitch," Blue Shirt snapped as he reached for the six-gun at his side.

With his left hand, Pike snapped the whiskey glass up and dashed the liquid into Blue Shirt's face, giving the man momentary pause. With his right, he ripped out a Colt and blasted the outlaw. As Blue Shirt was falling, the bounty hunter blasted Green Shirt, who had barely managed to get his pistol out of his holster.

Both men fell, Green Shirt dead, Blue Shirt not quite. He shakily tried to draw his pistol, but Pike kicked the weapon away.

There was a gunshot from behind him, and Pike dropped to one knee and spun. Out of the corner of his eye he saw the bartender crashing back onto the plank, sending bottles crashing to the floor. As he brought his Colt up, looking for whoever had fired the shot, he spotted Hastings, smoking pistol in hand.

"Emil?" Pike asked surprised and still wary.

"None other," the newly returned lawman said, sliding his own Colt away. He looked a little pasty.

Pike rose and did the same. "What're you doin' here?"

"Savin' your bacon. That bartender was about to plug you." He sounded a little shaky.

"Why?"

"Because he was going to kill you, dammit. I just told you that."

"No, why did you come back?"

"I just couldn't bear the thought of you considerin' me a coward," he said shakily.

"I didn't..."

"Donkey droppins." He was settling down a little. "I didn't get far, so I figured to come back and see if you needed help."

"I'm glad you did."

"Funny thing is, I didn't figure you'd need any. I figured you were just gonna shoot those boys down from the doorway."

"I considered it, but the thought of what a decent man—one who just got his tin star back—would say if I did that, and, well, I gave those boys a chance."

"Who...?" Hastings paused. "You mean me?"

Pike nodded once, then turned to face the few men who remained in the saloon. "You boys best head on out," Pike said. "Someone go tell Rupert I'll have some business here for him soon but tell him to keep out 'til I let him in. Marshal, guard the door. No one gets in without my say so."

"What's up, Brodie?" Hastings asked.

"One of 'em is still alive, and I plan to talk with him. I don't want anyone, includin' you, interfering while I'm doing so."

"But, Brodie..."

"Just do it, Emil."

The lawman shrugged and though irritated, took a place right outside the saloon door, which he closed behind him.

The bounty hunter knelt alongside the wounded man, who looked to be in some agony. "You may last a while, friend," Pike said, "and it'll likely be painful. Still, I'd be obliged if you were to answer some questions for me."

The man groaned, then asked, "I'm a dead man for sure, but I'd hate to go like this."

"You may bring tears to my eyes."

"But I'll talk to you if you promise to kill me instead of lettin' me die in pain this way."

Pike thought that over for a bit, then nodded. "It goes against my better judgment...what's your name?"

"Fleming."

"As I was saying, this goes against my grain when it comes to a man like you, Fleming. I'm sure what you tell me will not make me feel any better and will likely make me mad as hell. But if you talk to me, and tell the truth, I'll put you out of your misery. What happened to break that woman's spirit?" Pike feared what he figured he was going to hear, but he needed to hear it, to know for sure.

"She was a feisty one, that gal," Fleming said between coughs. "She took to orderin' Tink around since she figured it was her ranch and he was a hired hand sort of, even if he was her cousin. He took it for a few days, then smacked her, and kept smackin' her day after day. Taylor started doing so too. She fought back as best she could, though, but she was no match for them." He fell silent.

"Then?"

Fleming wheezed a little. "Taylor married her."

"She agree?"

"Don't know, but I doubt it. They paid some preacher a thousand dollars to perform the ceremony.

Paid the land office fella a thousand too, to make up the deed to the ranch.

"Promise me again that you'll kill me straight off."

"Why?"

"Because what I'm about to tell you will make you angrier than anything you've ever heard."

The thought of an eleven-year-old girl abused beyond belief flashed though his mind. "Ain't likely, though I reckon it'll come close." Pike clenched his teeth and took a few deep breaths. "I'll do so."

"The afternoon we come back from the marriage, Tink threw her down on the bed, tore her dress off, had a bunch of us hold her down, and took her. Then her 'husband' did, then the rest...of us did too."

Pike thought he would break bones in his hand, his fists were clenched so tight. His breathing was ragged.

"This went on most every day. After a few weeks it slacked off some, until it was just Tink and Taylor having her regularly. That broke her. She wasn't the same ever since."

Pike knelt there for more than a minute, trying to hold down his rage. Then he rose. "You are lucky, Fleming, very, very lucky that I'm a man of my word. If I weren't you'd die a most awful death." He pulled a Colt and shot Fleming in the head.

He turned and headed for the door, yanked it open, and steamed his way through the crowd.

Hastings hurried after him. "What'd you learn, Brodie?" the lawman asked nervously, hurrying to keep up with Pike.

"You don't want to know, Emil. You don't want to know."

"That bad?"

"Worse."

Hastings halted and stared at Pike fading into the dark.

CHAPTER TWENTY-FOUR

Pike and Hastings looked down at the once neat, trim house from a vantage point amid the pines. The place was some distance off, so they did not have a very good view, but it would have to do. They did not want to wander down into the valley and ride across the open ground between the hill and the house.

Beyond the structure was a large pasture with a bunch of dots. "Looks like a heap more cattle out there than when I was here that time a while ago," Pike said.

"You're right, and I'm sure Maggie didn't buy 'em all somewhere and drive 'em here."

"Yep."

"You been inside?"

"A couple times, not since Maggie got..."

"I was only in there that one time," Pike started. When he saw Hastings's dark mood, he added, "Dammit, Emil, stop it. You're gettin' to be a pain in my rump. Now, as I was sayin', I seem to recall that the only windows were those in front. That right?"

The marshal thought that over a few moments, then nodded.

"Well, we can get up close on the northeast side." Pike pointed. "The trees ain't far from there."

"What'll we do when we get there?"

"Hell if I know just yet. But maybe we can learn how many are in the house. If it's only one or two, we can probably pop in and take 'em before they realize what's going on."

"If there's more?"

"Then we skedaddle back up into the trees and try to figure out something else."

They made their way through the pines until they were opposite the northeast wall of the house, maybe twenty yards away. The outhouse was about halfway between where they were and the house. Leaving their horses tied to branches, they made their way down the slight slope. Just as they neared the outhouse, a man came out of the house and headed their way. The two ducked behind the shack. When the man went inside, Pike grabbed a substantial branch that someone had dropped when collecting firewood. He went and stood just beside the door.

The door opened, the man came out and walked two steps before Pike said, "Howdy." As the man turned, the bounty hunter slammed him across the chest with the branch. The man fell. Before he could shout an alarm, Pike placed a foot against his throat.

"How many men are in the house?" Pike asked.

"Two," the man said, his voice constricted with his throat under Pike's foot. "Taylor and Gus."

"Taylor Franks?" Hastings asked tightly.

"Yeah."

"Where are they in there?" Pike asked.

"They were sittin' at the table."

"Anything else you want to ask, Emil?"

"How's Maggie?"

"The woman? She's fine and dandy. Good little wife she is, takin' care of her husband and..."

His voice stopped when Pike pushed his boot down hard, crushing the man's windpipe, killing him. Seeing the marshal's anger growing, Pike warned, "Keep calm, Emil." He told himself the same thing silently.

They moved to the house and knelt at the side. Pike peeked around the corner but saw nothing. "Reckon the best I can do is kick the door in and blast away. If the two are at the table, it shouldn't be hard to take 'em down."

"Maggie's in there."

"Yep. I just hope she's not at the table."

"I don't like that idea, Brodie."

"Neither do I but I can't think of anything better."

"And what'll I be doing while you're blastin' away?"

"Finish things up if I ain't as good as I think I am. And be there for Maggie."

"If she's alive after you..."

"Hush," Pike whispered urgently. He peered around the corner again. Maggie was coming out of the house with a bucket in hand. She went down the three porch steps and headed across the yard to the well.

A man stepped outside and stood just outside the door on the porch. "Don't you dillydally, woman," the man said.

Pike grabbed Hastings's arm to keep him from charging out there. "Wait," he hissed. He looked around the corner. "Give me two seconds, then run like hell, grab Maggie and get her to safety behind the well or the trough."

Hastings nodded.

Pike drew a Colt, stepped around the corner of the porch, walked a few feet, then fired twice at the man near the door. Both slugs caught him in the side. Pike wasn't sure he had killed the man, but he charged up the steps and crouched to the side of the door.

Suddenly a shot rang out, crashing through the glass window. Pike heard a shriek from Maggie and glanced that way. Hastings had stumbled and gone down to one knee, then rose. With their arms around each other, he and Maggie ran for the well as another shot kicked up dirt to the marshal's right.

Pike yanked the other Colt out in his left hand, stuck his arm around the door jamb and fired off four rounds at where he thought the gunman was. Then he charged inside, both Colts ready. But the revolvers were not needed. Somehow Pike had managed to hit the gunman twice, once in the side and once in the head. He knew it was pure luck. He checked the other man, but he was dead too.

Finally, he stepped outside and down the steps. "Emil," he called, "Maggie. It's Brodie. There's no more danger here."

The two stood and walked toward Pike. "How bad?" the bounty hunter asked, pointing to the blood on the lawman's shirt.

"I'll be all right. It hurts like all hellfire but it didn't hit anything vital."

Pike nodded. "You okay, Maggie?"

"Yes," she said, head down, her voice barely a whisper.

"What did you say?" Pike demanded.

"I said yes." There was no more volume in her voice.

"Look at me, girl," Pike snapped.

"Now wait a minute, Brodie," Hastings started.

"Shut up, Emil. I said look at me, girl."

She did, her face a mask of fear and worry, of exhaustion and resignation.

"First time I saw you, Maggie," Pike said in a calmer tone, "you were as feisty as a spirited horse. I know what you've been through."

"How do...?"

"Doesn't matter how I know. I do. It must have been horrible, worse than horrible. But there's no reason to be ashamed. You were forced into this by a small army of men, scum, they are the lowest of the low. Now it's over and it's time for the real Maggie to come out again."

"I can't." She hung her head again.

"Pardon my language, Maggie, but the hell you

can't. Shameful things were done to you, there's no denyin' that. But you ain't a mouse. You're a tough woman deep down. You showed that when I rode up those months ago and you greeted me with a shotgun —and the gumption to use it if you had to. And you showed it when Sykes and his scum tried to take you. You didn't let those fellas break you, and you shouldn't let what these ones have done break your spirit. Ain't many women, maybe, who can overcome the evil that's been done to you. But I'm layin' my money on you, Maggie. It's over, and the real Maggie needs to show her face again."

"I ain't sure she's still in there." She glanced at Hastings, who stood with gritted teeth. "Not after what they...they...did."

"Doesn't matter what they did. I know it was awful, beyond awful. But the real Maggie is still in there, inside you. Take Emil there. He didn't suffer near what you have, but he was humiliated by those men and fell into a hole he never thought he'd get out of. But he did. He's a brave, good man, strong inside. You're strong inside too."

"But Emil won't want me. Not after I been shamed so much."

"Then to hell with Emil." Despite his anger, Pike almost smiled at the pained look on Hastings's face. "You don't need him or anybody else. You were runnin' this ranch, or at least ready to, by yourself as best I can figure. You can do so again. You just open up and let that tough ol' gal come roarin' out. Emil don't like what you been forced into, that's his trouble. Not yours. It ain't gonna be easy for you. I ain't saying it'll be, and you can't forget what happened. But maybe you can put it aside. It'll take time for sure, but you're strong enough—and excuse my language again—to kick what those bastards have done to you into a hole in the ground. It might take a long time to cover that hole up, but you damn well can do it."

Maggie's head rose and a look of determination settled on her face. She nodded.

"Good. Emil, can you saddle a horse with that hole in your shoulder?"

"I ain't sure."

"I can," Maggie said.

"You'll have to ride astride."

"Don't even have one. Astride's the only way I ride. I can't abide a sidesaddle, and out here they're a hindrance."

"Good. Go on and saddle one for you. I'll get our horses and bring 'em down here."

Maggie had a horse saddled and was waiting in the yard next to Hastings when Pike rode up towing the lawman's animal behind him. He handed the reins to Hastings, who mounted with little trouble.

"I want you two to get to Nederland as fast as you can. Emil, you head straight to a doctor. You know anyone in town, Maggie, who can watch over you?"

"I don't need watching over," she said tightly. "I'm a tough ol' gal, remember?"

Pike nodded. "Well, someone you trust who can put you up for a few days?"

"If she doesn't know anyone, I do," Hastings said quietly, almost as if afraid to speak.

"Good. You gonna be all right, Emil?"

The lawman looked stricken but nodded tightly. "At least for now, I reckon."

"What're you gonna do?" Maggie asked.

"Take care of the rest of those sons a...um, outlaws."

"You'll be alone," Maggie said.

"I've been alone before."

"But there's eight or nine of 'em here besides those..." She shuddered. "And there's a few more in town."

"The ones in town won't be botherin' anyone ever again."

Maggie looked at Hastings, who nodded.

"Where are the ones not in town?"

"Hard to remember after what..."

"I know, but you can do it."

Maggie thought a moment. Two of 'em are out in the pasture keeping watch on the herd. Two others are heading out there to relieve them of that duty. A couple are out rustlin' more cattle. Or so they said. They might be doing something else."

"Like what?"

"I'm not sure. I heard the men talking about robbing a stage between Nederland and Black Hawk or maybe Central City. There's one or two more men I can't account for."

"Where's Tink?"

"In Boulder. He was supposed to meet some more men there."

"Thanks."

Pike helped Maggie onto her horse. "Don't be too

hard on Emil, Maggie. He needs time too, and maybe there'll never be enough."

Maggie mounted and rode up alongside Pike, who was on the sorrel. "I will. And thank you, Brodie."

"No need to thank me. And I wasn't alone." He nodded toward Hastings. "Don't delay, you two."

CHAPTER TWENTY-FIVE

A few yards on, Pike stopped. He turned and watched Hastings and Maggie riding away down the road through the gap between the hills. Once again, he cursed himself for bringing trouble on these two people. If it weren't for him, Maggie Donovan would never have been forced into a loathsome marriage and lost her ranch. If he hadn't interfered, Marshal Emil Hastings would not have been wounded. He knew deep inside that it wasn't true. Had he not intervened, Maggie likely would be dead after having been ravaged by Tink Conroy and his gang, and Hastings would still be riding full tilt down rotgut road. But, still, as usual, he thought the worst of himself.

"Bah," he finally muttered and headed for the foothills northeast of the ranch house.

Pike kicked the gelding into a run and veered left up the slope before he neared the pasture. A few minutes later, from up on the hill, leaning against a pine, he pulled out his telescope and surveyed the pasture before him. Nearest him, about thirty head of cattle grazed complacently. They were not bunched too closely, but they weren't spread out too far either. At the far side of the pasture four men on horseback talked among themselves, keeping a desultory eye on the animals.

He swept the landscape a few times, searching for any sign that the man or men Maggie couldn't account for were in the area, but he saw nothing. That concerned him.

He remained there for a few more minutes, trying to formulate a plan. He had come up with the beginnings of one when he spotted movement to the southwest. Two men were coming out of the foothills on that side of the ranch, heading slowly toward the house.

"Damn," Pike muttered. He was divided. He could try to take care of those two, then hope to take down the others or he could try to rid the earth of the ones in the pasture before going after the two heading for the house. Once those two discovered the bodies, all hell would break loose. Gunshots at either group would alert the other, and that could scatter the men, making them harder to catch.

He sighed, wishing he had his sniper rifle. He thought now that leaving it with Charlie McAllister for safekeeping might have been a mistake.

"Well, make up your mind, Brodie. You've been in worse spots before."

Deciding, Pike mounted the gelding and headed down the hill. Two would be easier to face than four, so he would start here, creating a diversion that would keep the four distracted while he went after the two who were headed toward the house.

Three of the four men were still a little too far off for Pike to use his Henry. He might get one, if lucky, but the others would scatter. The fourth one had drifted nearer to him though still on the far side of the small herd, but he was close enough for a shot. Even if he missed, it should trigger a stampede. He just hoped it worked. If not, he could be in big trouble.

Halfway down the hill, he dismounted, lightly tied the horse to a branch, and pulled out the Henry. Kneeling, he took aim at the guard and fired. Before the smoke had cleared, before he knew whether he had hit his target, he was back in the saddle and racing toward the herd. He could vaguely see that the man he had shot was reeling in the saddle. Then, with a yell, he fired the rifle several times.

Pike swung the horse back and forth behind the herd, shouting at the top of his lungs and firing a few more times. It took a few moments longer than he had hoped, given him momentary pause, but the animals moved off, slowly at first, then gathering speed until they were in a full stampede. Pike rode behind, still urging the cattle to keep moving. He saw that the horse the man he had shot had been on, was racing off riderless.

Within a minute, he pulled to the side, out of the cloud of dust that threatened his eyesight and had come close to clogging his throat.

Through the brownish curtain, he could see the

other three men frantically trying to stem the stampede, fighting to turn the animals back upon themselves. Pike figured they would be busy for a spell, so he would have time to keep an eye out for the two men who were off rustling more cattle and wait to ambush the ones he had seen riding toward the cabin. They would have heard the shots and would be hightailing it toward the pasturage.

He headed east across the pasture and up the hill to a vantage point where he could watch the low, wide gap through the foothills between the house and the pasture. He barely had time to reload the Henry before he saw two men riding hell-bent for the pasture. They were too far out from him to make hitting them unlikely, so he galloped down off the hill and waited roughly in the center of the gap.

The two men did not slow when they saw him, figuring he was one of their companions. He dismounted, rifle in hand, then dropped to one knee and fired. One horse was hit in the chest and went down, sliding on the grass, throwing its rider. Pike was luckier with the next two shots, plugging the other man, who toppled from his horse, which kept running.

Pike vaulted back into the saddle and raced toward the man who had been thrown by the dead horse and was struggling to rise. He glanced at the one he had shot, satisfying himself that the outlaw was dead. He stopped and looked down at the surviving man. "Howdy. You have a choice. Surrender and let me tie you up back at the house until I take care of your friends and then bring you—and them, if they have any sense—back to Nederland. The only other option is to die where you stand."

"Maybe I'll just surrender," the man said with a smirk. "I won't be indisposed long before my friends come and kill you and set me free. You might not even make it to the house. The boys inside will take care of you."

"Did you look inside?"

"Nope." Uncertainty crept into the man's voice. "Didn't have time."

"Well, then, if I were you, I wouldn't count on getting any help from the boys there. Dead men can't be of much help."

"You're lyin'."

"You came runnin' this way because you heard the gunshots, I presume. Have any of the men from the house joined you?" Without taking his eyes off the outlaw, Pike put the Henry in the scabbard.

Worry crept across the man's face. "How do I know you won't kill me once I'm trussed up?" he asked, worry deep in his voice.

"That'd waste my time. If I wanted to shoot you, I would've done so." He paused a moment to let that sink in. "Now, you have five seconds to make your choice."

The man licked his lips, then went for his revolver.

Even if he had not been slowed by being thrown from his dead horse, he would have been no match for the bounty hunter, who drew a Colt and plugged the outlaw twice in the chest.

Shaking his head at the foolishness of some men, he turned and rode back to where the herd was. The riders were struggling to quiet the nervous animals. One of the men was at the front of the herd, still trying to get the beasts to circle in on themselves. The other two were on the left flank, trying to calm the animals.

Pike grinned maliciously, pulled the Henry, and fired three times, once at the outlaw nearest him, the other two into the ground near the rear of the herd. The already fractious animals dashed forth anew. The rider in front darted toward the foothills to the west, his horse carrying him out of danger and needing no urging.

The outlaw Pike had shot at glanced over his shoulder. He was unhit but had heard the shots that had sent the cattle stampeding again. He shouted to his nearest companion, and both quickly joined their comrade in galloping toward the hills slightly to the northwest.

Pike charged after the three outlaws but bolted into the woods before they did so farther ahead.

Minutes later, Pike crested another hill that led to a small valley. He caught a glimpse of his quarry still racing over another crest. He pressed on, over two more hills, then from the top of another he spotted three men crossing the glen. He stopped and reached for the Henry, but paused, realizing the men were heading toward him not away from him. And they were in no hurry. He let the gelding pick itself down the hill and onto the grass, then moved forward. He stopped about five yards from where the three men had come to a halt. He had a hand on the butt of one of his Colts.

"You boys seen three fellas ridin' hell-bent this way?"

"No, sir," one man, who appeared to be in charge said. He and the other two looked nervous. "Why?"

"Searchin' for 'em."

The leader stiffened his back. "Why?"

"Stop their outlawry."

"Not join 'em?"

The bounty hunter smiled. "Nope I aim to put an end to their crimes."

The man relaxed a bit and said, "You don't have a badge."

"Don't need one. I find 'em, they'll either surrender and let me take 'em back to face justice or I'll take 'em back over their saddles." Pike paused. "And who are you?"

"Blue Weatherby. Fellow on the right is Stan Barker. And this is," he nodded at the man next to him, "is John Wilkins."

Pike nodded. "Where's the stage route from here through Rollinsville to Black Hawk?"

Weatherby looked at him quizzically. "Why?"

"I think two more of those boys were plannin' to rob the stage."

"You going after them too?"

"Yep."

"Pretty long odds if the three you're chasin' meet up with the other two."

"Yep."

"Don't that worry you?"

"Worry? No. But cautious for sure." He paused. "The road?"

Weatherby hesitated, then chucked a thumb over his shoulder. "Over that hill there, then about five miles southwest. Follow the stream for another mile or so and across the hill to the south."

"How would they get from that road to Maggie Donovan's place?"

"That cattle rustlin' whore," Barker started but stopped when he saw Pike's face cloud with anger.

"One more word of such filth comes out of your mouth, boy, I'll fill you so full of holes you'll sound like a tin whistle when the wind blows. Miz Donovan is a good woman who was forced into a mighty bad situation by some foul men who ain't fit to walk on the same ground as..." He slammed to a stop.

"I'm sorry, Mister," Barker said, voice full of contrition. "We didn't know. We...It was her place and..."

Pike nodded and looked back at Weatherby. "The trail?"

"When you hit that road, follow it north. About six miles up, there's a fork. Take the one to the west. That'll lead you right to her place. When you enter the gap between two low hills, you're almost there."

Pike nodded again. After a moment, he asked, "What're you boys doing out here?"

"Looking for rustled cattle. One of the other ranchers followed the trail for a while and said it seemed to lead straight to Miz Donovan's place. We were hopin' that at least a few of 'em had wandered off back toward home. We didn't think we'd have any success, but we had to try something. I've lost seven head, and John four. I lose one or two more—and I don't have many more than that—and I won't be able to feed the family." He grinned tightly. "Or pay Stan here."

"I doubt you'll find any loose cattle, and I'd advise you to turn back and go on home. I think those boys are about done with rustlin'."

"Why's that?"

"I believe they have other crimes—more profitable ones—in mind."

"I don't give a damn about them or anyone else committing

any kind of crimes. Except one. Not when I'm faced with the loss of everything I own because of rustlers."

"Understandable. But you'd possibly be facin' five, six hardened gunmen," Pike said not entirely truthfully, having lessened the odds a bit. "Like I said, I think they're done rustlin'. And if I stop 'em like I plan on doin'..."

"By yourself?" Weatherby asked, skeptical.

"I'll have some help," Pike lied. "I'll come by or send someone to let you know things are all right. Again, I suggest you boys head home and wait things out."

"And if you don't say everything's all right?"

"Then you're on your own."

Weatherby sat in thought for a moment, worried, then nodded. "Reckon you're right. Good luck in your hunt. You'll likely need it." He and the others turned their horses and rode back the way they had come from.

Pike watched until the three men were mere specks on the horizon, then headed toward the stage road.

CHAPTER TWENTY-SIX

Before long, Pike stopped and considered the situation. Daylight was fast fading and he believed, though he did not know why, that the outlaws had finished their dirty work and likely had returned to Maggie's. Or were on their way. He was sure they would remain there for some time, so if he missed them on the road, he could catch them there. That he did not know where the three he had originally been chasing were or whether they had joined up with these two robbers made his decision easier.

He found a trickle of water nearby, unsaddled the gelding and let him drink, then he hobbled him and left him to graze. He had no food, really, so he had to be content with a few pieces of jerky and water. Before long, he stretched out in his bedroll and was quickly asleep.

Still, he was not very well rested when he awoke and with his breakfast being solely jerky and water, his humor was not good. Angrily he saddled the horse, attached his bedroll to the cantle, mounted, and headed to the trail that would lead to the gap near the small ranch.

A few hours later, he got to the passage and stopped, not wanting to just ride out into the open. He didn't think the men—if they were here—would be watching for anyone coming from there, but he thought it foolish to take the risk. He backtracked a little, to where the slope of the hill on one side was not nearly as steep and forced the horse up through the trees.

Pike stopped near the top and tied the gelding to a spruce, then crept forward. Leaning against a tree, he pulled out his collapsible telescope and surveyed the area. He was surprised to see that there was no one watching over the herd, but with the pasture surrounded by hills and mountains except for a small area near the house, they would go nowhere.

He could not see much of the house from where he was, but he did notice that the bodies of the three men he had killed when he and Hastings has rescued Maggie, were gone. He wondered if the outlaws were still there or if they had moved on, leaving the cattle. "Well, there's one way to find out," he muttered as he closed the telescope in on itself and headed toward the horse.

He rode along the ridge and then down the slope of the hill to the side of the barn away from the house. He tied the gelding to a hackberry bush that had survived the barn's construction and slipped inside the building. He found fourteen horses crammed into the barn, four or five to a stall, and almost as many saddles draped over the walls of the few stalls. He figured three for the men he had killed in the house, the four who had been guarding the cattle, three of whom apparently were here, two for the men he had shot racing back to the herd from the house, and two for the robbers who had been away. The other three were likely just extras, though he worried a little that the outlaws might have gotten reinforcements. Even if they hadn't, he still faced five men, seven if the man or men that Maggie couldn't account for were here.

He stood leaning against the door jamb, mostly in the shadows making it difficult for anyone in the house to see him, watching over the small domicile, and considered what to do next. His choices seemed limited.

Just charging through the door of the house as he had done several times before in his career as a bounty hunter did not appeal to him. At least one time he did that, he took three bullets. He could, he supposed, try to burn the outlaws out but he was reluctant for some reason to try to do so. He considered waiting the men out. All of them would have to come outside at some point. He could, he thought, take them out one by one, but that would mean doing so with knife or bare hands. Using a firearm would alert the others and have them hunkering down inside making it even more difficult to take care of them. Besides, once one or two of the men did not return, others would come looking for them.

Still undecided, he brought the gelding inside and loosened the cinch on the sorrel. He pulled two horses from one stall, tying them to a post, then led the gelding into it. He found some apples and carrots, which he tossed in a trough and let the gelding eat. He went back to his spot at the barn door.

Pike snapped to attention when he saw a man coming out of the house and heading toward him. He slipped inside the barn and grabbed a Winchester from the first saddle he saw, and then stationed himself just inside the doorway to one side.

The man entered and Pike stepped up and swung the rifle like a club. The stock splattered the outlaw's face, and he sank to the ground without a sound. The man was still alive, though not by much. Pike figured that even if he roused himself a little, he would not be able to do anything because of his smashed face.

Pike decided it was time to do something. He didn't know what yet, but he could no longer just stand around doing nothing. He had to force the issue somehow. He went back and tightened the sorrel's cinch, so the animal was ready if he needed him. Then he began letting the outlaws' horses out of the stalls. He pushed them toward the wide barn door, then slapped a riding quirt on the rumps of the last couple of animals. The horses bolted, streaming wildly out of the barn.

He grabbed the Henry from the scabbard and ran back to the door. Outlaws were boiling out of the house. Smiling grimly, Pike brought the Henry to his shoulder and fired, levered in another round, fired again, and again.

Two men went down, likely killed. Another spun as if hit but did not fall.

The others looked around, wondering what

happened but with all the noise, dust, and confusion, they could not see Pike. Still, they knew something was wrong. Three of them, including the wounded man, dashed back into the house; the other two headed up the hill into the trees, using the horses as shields as best they could.

"Damn," the bounty hunter muttered. He didn't know what he had expected to happen, but this development was not good. He shook his head in annoyance and looked out past the door. He figured the men in the house would stay put. The others might do anything—run for town, try to catch some horses and flee, try to make their way around to the back of the house then find a way to join their fellows inside.

He decided to go after the two on foot. He would decide what to do about the men in the house later. He mounted the gelding, stuck the Henry in the scabbard, left the barn, and turned to put the building between him and the house. He rode up the hill into the trees and turned left, picking his way carefully through the pines. When he was about in a straight line to the center of the house across the road leading to the yard, he dismounted and tied his horse to a tree. He patted him on the neck, then drifted off, creeping toward his left.

Suddenly a bullet slammed into a tree, sending shards of bark over his face. Another tore through the side of his shirt, barely nicking him. "Damn," he snapped quietly as he hit the ground. Another bullet, this one from a different direction, sizzled a thin line across the side of his neck.

He flopped onto his back and pushed with his

boots, scooting behind a thick-trunked pine a few feet from where he had been. He stood, his back scraping along the bark. Two bullets flew toward the tree where he had been moments before. One hit the tree lower than the previous one; the other dug up some dirt near the bottom.

Pike caught a glimpse of lingering gunsmoke in the air a few yards to his right. Judging by where the other bullets had come from, he had some idea where the other outlaw was. He pulled one of his Colts and crouching, slipped from one tree to another, heading to where he had seen the smoke, planning to come up behind the man. He was within a few feet when the outlaw sensed him. The man spun, falling backward as he fired twice. One bullet sizzled harmlessly by Pike's head; the other tore out small pieces of Pike's shirt and shoulder.

The bounty hunter fired twice, missing with both shots as the outlaw scrabbled backward. A third shot caught the man high on the chest, a fourth hit him in the throat. As Pike cautiously crept up on the man uncertain if the fellow was dead, he heard a crashing along the pine needles as the other outlaw ran.

"Damn," Pike muttered again when he realized the man was heading to where Pike's gelding was. Noting with a glance that the outlaw lying before him was dead, he rushed toward the sound.

The man had grabbed the reins to the sorrel from the branch where it was tied and leaped onto the horse. The animal shuffled some, not liking the unfamiliar rider. When the man kicked his spurs into the horse's flanks, the gelding reared, unused to having jagged metal tear into his flesh. The outlaw, who had not gotten his feet into the stirrups because they were too long for him tumbled off the back of the gelding, who dashed off.

Pike, who had been trying unsuccessfully to get a bead on the man, rushed up as the man hit the ground. "Son of a..." he growled. He stomped a boot heel on the outlaw's face, shattering it, sending shards of bone into the brain.

Pike stood there reloading the Colt and slipping it back into the holster. He felt his neck and saw that the blood that came away with his fingers was almost dry already. He waited, hoping the gelding would return, which it did after enough time that Pike had begun to worry.

"That's a good boy," the bounty hunter said, gently patting the horse on the neck. "Wish I had an apple or something for you. I'll get you some soon as I can." The horse snuffled its approval.

"Well, Brodie," Pike thought aloud, "what're you gonna do about those boys in the house?" He had no answer for himself. He grabbed the gelding's reins and walked, towing the horse, to a spot where he was almost directly across from the house's front door. He tied the horse to a branch, took his Henry and telescope and checked out the structure. He could see nothing that might help him. With a sigh, he sat.

"You sure as hell blundered this time, old boy," he mumbled. The men in the house could hold out for a long time, he was sure. He figured they had ample supplies of food, coffee, and more. Pike had nothing but some water in a canteen and some strips of jerky.

His only hope was that the outlaws had little water inside and would have to try to get to the well. Of course, Pike thought, they could wait 'til dark to do so. They'd also have to use the privy, though the bounty hunter suspected they outlaws would not bother and just relieve themselves on the floor or something. So Pike waited.

Before long, some of the horses began wandering back into the yard. They stopped at the trough and drank, then placidly drifted off to find fodder, seemingly content.

Half a lifetime—or maybe just a couple of hours—later, the door opened, and a man tentatively shuffled out. He stood on the porch a bit, head swiveling from side to side as he tried to spot any possible trouble.

Up on the hill, Pike raised the Henry, took aim, and then put the rifle back down. If he did nothing, the outlaws might figure he was either dead or had run off.

The man on the porch said something over his shoulder to those inside then stepped into the yard, heading for one of the horses. The two other men followed.

Pike smiled grimly and raised the rifle. He fired, then again and again, seven times in all. Pike hit one man in the chest and side, fired five more times, hitting one man twice in the chest, one in the head, the other once in the stomach. The other slugs kicked up dirt. The horses scattered again.

The bounty hunter got the gelding, put the rifle into the scabbard, mounted and rode slowly down the hill. He stopped and looked down at the man he had shot in the chest. He was dead. As were the others.

The bounty hunter cared for the sorrel and made sure the animal had feed and water, then headed toward the house. Halfway across the yard, he stopped. Then with a sigh, he started dragging the corpses around to the back of the house, where he found the three he had taken care of in Maggie's rescue. Finally, he went inside, tiredness overtaking him.

Shaking off the exhaustion, he found some cold fried chicken and some bread that had been fresh a day or two ago. He ate without enthusiasm, then went to the barn and got the materials for cleaning his weapons. He started with the Henry, then went on to his Colts, one at a time, always keeping the other loaded and ready.

Pike was looking at the bed and contemplating a decent night's sleep when he heard horses. He figured it was just more of the horses that he had scattered earlier drifting back. Until he looked out the window. Five men were riding into the yard. Twenty yards from the house, they stopped and spread out.

"Gus?" one man called out. "Barber?"

Pike recognized the man from the description Maggie had given him, as Tink Conroy. The bounty hunter started for the door, dropping the Henry on the table before opening the door and stepping out onto the porch. He knew this was a foolish idea, but there had been enough killing, if he could prevent more.

"Howdy, boys," he said with mock warmth.

"Who the hell are you?" Conroy demanded.

"The man who's gonna put an end to your rustlin' and thievin'."

Conroy laughed. "You got some nerve, boy. Now why don't you..."

Pike ignored him, instead addressing his four companions. "I don't know what this villain has told you or offered you, but whatever it is ain't worth dyin' for."

"Mighty big statement for a man alone against five."

"I wasn't talkin' to you, Tink, so shut your trap. All the men who've ridden with this son of a bitch are dead. You will join them unless you drop your weapons and ride out of here."

"Hell, you couldn't have killed 'em all, boy," Conroy snapped.

"Well, that's true I haven't killed 'em all," Pike said with a small nod. "You're left, and I'll take care of you soon's I deal with these other fellas."

"Mr. Conroy's right," one of the men said, "you do have some stones on you, Mister. You expect us to believe you killed all his men?"

"Yep. All thirteen, or was it fourteen, of 'em."

The newcomers guffawed. "Good story, Mister," Conroy said.

"Did any of your men greet you in Nederland? How many of 'em are here to greet you now? You can find a heap of 'em piled up in back of the house."

Conroy seemed to fume and was unable to say anything.

Pike's hands inched toward his Colts. "Time to

make up your minds boys. Leave and live or stay with this scum and die." While the five men were laughing, Pike eased his revolvers out. By the time the newcomers were aware that the bounty hunter had his six-guns in hand, two were dead, a third wounded, and a fourth fighting his nervously prancing horse. Conroy was sitting there tightly holding the reins of his mount, keeping it rather steady.

Pike shot the former, then slowly walked toward Conroy. The outlaw had dropped the reins and was going for his revolver, but Pike shot him in the thigh, then yanked him off his horse. Conroy pulled a revolver and shakily pointed it at Pike. He fired, the bullet grazing Pike's upper arm. Before he could fire again, Pike kicked the weapon away.

Another shot rang out, slicing a furrow across Pike's side. He spun and fired the last two rounds in his revolvers. The outlaw slumped in the saddle, and his horse took off.

Pike put a boot on Conroy's chest and held him there while he reloaded his Colts. Then he knelt at the outlaw's side.

You've caused a heap of trouble for some good people, Mr. Conroy. I cannot abide such a thing. Unless you..." He suddenly spun and fired his Colt, putting a bullet into the chest of the man he had wounded earlier, but not before the outlaw had hit him in the side, cracking a rib. He got some rope from one of the outlaws' horses that had wandered back into the area.

CHAPTER TWENTY-SEVEN

Pike rolled Conroy over on his stomach and tied his hands behind his back. He cut the length of rope off, then rolled him back over.

"You're not gonna kill me?" the outlaw asked, surprised.

"Nope. That'd be too good for the likes of you. I'm gonna take you back to Nederland."

Conroy grinned. "I got boys there that'll take care of you."

"No, you don't, if you remember that you got no greeting when you were there earlier today."

The outlaw looked at Pike, fear suddenly growing in his eyes. Then he got hold of himself. "Hell, Maggie'll see to it that I go free."

"You best hope someone puts a rope around Maggie. If she's not bound up, she might just take to gettin' a knife and carvin' you up."

"That meek little chippie?"

"I think you'll be surprised at how meek she ain't

anymore." He unsaddled the gelding, led him to the trough and then to the barn where he made sure the horse had plenty of grain. Then he headed back to the house.

Conroy had been shouting the whole time, and Pike was tired of it. "Mr. Conroy, I aim to feed myself and I hope you'll be quiet while I make me something to eat."

He took the rest of the rope, placed a slipknot around Conroy's neck, then tied that to a hitching rail alongside the porch. Conroy could do little more than lie there on his back. "Sit tight."

"Hey, you son of a bitch, come back here and set me free!" the outlaw screeched.

Pike came back down the steps. "Like I said, I'd like to eat my supper—or is it lunch? Well, no matter—in peace, so I'd be obliged if you kept your mouth shut."

"You'll get no quiet out of me, you bastard."

The bounty hunter let out an exaggerated sigh and kicked Conroy in the head. It didn't knock him out, but it was close to it. Pike walked back inside.

An hour later, he came back out, stomach full. The various small wounds had calmed, and he was in a much better humor than before. At least until he looked at Tink Conroy. "Damn," he whispered. He went to the barn and saddled the gelding. It took a little time and effort, but he finally grabbed one of the outlaws' horses and saddled it too. He hauled Conroy up by his shirtfront. "You can ride astride or hanging over the saddle. Which is it?"

"Astride," Conroy gargled.

Pike helped Conroy onto the horse. The rope was still around the outlaw's neck and his hands still tied.

The outlaw spit at Pike, the spittle landing on his hat. The bounty hunter punched Conroy in his wounded leg, and the outlaw hissed in pain.

"There's more of that if you'd like," Pike said as he tied the rope around the man's neck to the saddle horn, then tied his legs under the horse's belly. He mounted the gelding and rode off, the reins to Conroy's horse in his hand.

A couple hours later, they rode into Nederland. Someone had seen them coming and had alerted the town and a crowd was gathering. Marshal Emil Hastings and Maggie hurried up. Hastings held back a little way.

"Tink!" Maggie gasped, suddenly looking a bit fearful.

"Yep. This dumb bastard thinks I done something wrong. All I did was find you a decent young man."

Maggie looked close to tears. "He was scum. And he and you stole my ranch," she blubbered.

"Hell, you didn't deserve it anyway." Conroy said with a smarmy grin.

"Maggie," Pike said softly. When she looked at him, he said, "If you hit just the right spot on that wounded leg there, he'll likely change his attitude."

Maggie looked as if she was going to argue meekly, then smiled, perking up. She stepped up to the side of the outlaw's horse and pointed. "Right here?"

"That'd do."

Maggie reared back and hit Conroy on his wound

with all the strength she could muster in her slight body.

Conroy grunted with the pain and spit at the woman, hitting her bonnet.

She flushed in anger and embarrassment.

"I think he needs another attitude adjustment."

With determination, the woman punched him again.

Once more the outlaw simply grunted, showing little of the pain he might be feeling.

"Guess I ain't strong enough, Brodie," Maggie said sadly.

"That you ain't, girl," Conroy said with a slimy laugh.

Once more the woman looked close to tears, but she turned to face Pike when he said, "This might help." He held out his large, sharp knife.

"I couldn't."

"Yes you can." Pike nodded.

Determination returned anew to her face and she took the blade. She turned.

"Don't you do it, girl," Conroy said with bravado. "A good woman wouldn't do such a thing. But I reckon you ain't a good woman after you were whorin' around with..."

He shut up in a hurry when Maggie, wide-eyed in anger, jammed the point of the knife into the ragged bullet hole.

Conroy screamed. Most of the men in the crowd gasped. So did some of the women. Some other females smiled, perhaps hiding it behind a hand, in approval.

Maggie reared back to have another go, but Pike said, "Higher."

Maggie nodded and plunged the knife into Conroy's thigh, high up, getting a little close to the groin.

Once more she went to stab her cousin, but Pike said, "That's enough, Maggie."

The woman turned, angry, and hesitated, then nodded and handed the knife back to Pike.

"You all right, Brodie?" Hastings asked. "You got blood all over you."

"Just some scratches. You don't look so bad."

"Doc said it wasn't much. And Maggie's been taking care of me a little," his face red with embarrassment. He pointed to Conroy. "What do we do with him?"

"You best get me to a doc first thing," the outlaw snapped.

Everyone ignored him.

"First off, we go to that poor excuse of a preacher and have him annul that false marriage, if it was legal in the first place. Then we go to the land office and have him deed the ranch back to Maggie. We'll take him along in case we need him to spell things out to those culprits."

"I ain't helpin' none of you."

Everyone ignored him.

"Then what?" Hastings asked.

"Then you throw him in the hoosegow, after you clean up what's left of Magruder."

"I don't have jurisdiction over the ranch."

"Stop being an ass, Emil. I brought him in and

you're keepin' him jailed until I can get him to Golden for the reward. Besides, I don't think he'll be in there long."

Hastings looked around when he heard a growling murmur from the crowd. "I see what you mean, Brodie. Well, let's go talk to the preacher."

They finished up their business with the preacher, who turned out to not be a preacher, and the land office. Then they went the short distance to what passed as a marshal's office and jail, where Pike dismounted and helped Conroy down from his horse. They hustled the outlaw inside and chained him to the log, which two men had lifted off Magruder's chest and then hauled the body away.

"Enjoy your stay," Pike said with a grin. "However long—or short—it might be."

"I just remembered," Pike said, "you need to send someone out to Blue Weatherby's place. I told him I'd let him know when things were clear so he could go get his cattle. He can tell the others. If he's an honest man."

"He is. I'll get someone to head out there right off."

"Tell them to cull out their own cattle and leave Maggie's alone. If you know someone in town you can trust and knows what he's doin', send him out to watch over Maggie's place and keep an eye on her animals. Unless you know someone else who might want that job."

Hastings looked confused for a few moments. Pike stared at him, and the marshal nodded.

"Oh, and tell him he'll have to take care of a pile of

bodies behind the house. Nothing fancy, just dig a hole and put 'em all in one."

* * *

Conroy's stay in the jail, as predicted, wasn't long. That night, while Hastings took a long, leisurely supper with Maggie and Pike, a meal that was uncomfortable for all of them, some person or persons unknown, many of whom had suffered at the hands of Conroy's men, gave the outlaw a fine necktie party. The marshal, bounty hunter, and woman expressed a faux surprise when they saw the outlaw dangling from a tree after they had finished their food.

Conroy was buried the next morning unceremoniously a mile outside of town.

* * *

Three days later, Pike, Hastings, and Maggie met again at the restaurant, this time for breakfast, also an uncomfortable meal, especially for Pike. Over the past few days, Maggie had tried to spend as much time as she could with the bounty hunter, it seemed, and neither he nor Hastings liked it.

"Do you have to leave, Brodie?" Maggie asked wistfully.

"Yes."

"But why. I…"

"Maggie," Hastings said sadly, "I know I ain't come to grips with what's happened, but you wantin' to go with Brodie is foolish. I know you have feelins for

Brodie. But I got feelins for you, which you know. And I don't know if Brodie has feelins for you. I expect he doesn't, at least in the way you want."

"He's right, Maggie. You hardly know me, but you know Emil. He's a good man. He'll make you a fine husband."

"Not when he can't deal with my past."

"He'll come around," Pike said with more confidence than he felt.

"But I can make you love me, Brodie. I'm not so sure about Emil. If he really loved me, things would be different. But they're not. I know it ain't been but a few days, but there's been no change in him. I also think it'd be good for me to get away from here. All these folks know that I'm tainted. Going with you will get me away from that."

"My kind of life is not for you or any good woman, Maggie."

"There are many folk here who don't think I'm a decent woman anymore, Brodie. Some women want a life of adventure," Maggie said. "I'm not sure if I'm one of 'em. The thought of a wild life sounds appealing in some ways. Too frightening in others. A stable life with a family is also appealing. So I just can't decide."

"You got your ranch back, Maggie, but you can't really believe that this man," Hastings said, pointing at Pike, "will settle down and become a small-time rancher, do you?"

"He...I think so."

"No, Maggie," Pike said softly. "Emil's right. Like I said, a woman like you—any decent woman—would lose their mind within a few days of ridin' with me. Or at least within a few days of the first time we ran into some outlaws I was chasin' and gunfire broke out. My first wife…" He took a deep breath and let it out. "No, Maggie, this life ain't for a decent woman. Never settlin' down in one place for more than a few days. Rough camps in the wild, rougher men to face, poor food and often not enough of it, too many hours on a horse. Even worse, if I were to lose against some of these bad men, you'd be at their mercy. I had thought for a time—well, more like wished—that it could be so." He smiled sadly. "Even a fella like me dreams now and again of settlin' down, especially when he meets a fine woman like you. But even if I was able to settle down like that, things'd turn out bad. Trouble, gunfire, and death follow me around like winter follows fall. No, it'd never work."

"But, Brodie, we…"

"Like I said, Maggie, we hardly know each other. You'll be much better off with Emil, who I think will come around. And you do favor him more than a little." He clapped his hat on his head. "And you, Marshal, best make up your mind and damned soon. Let a decent woman go because of her past, a past she didn't ask for, or marry her—if she'll have you after the way you've been actin'. She's startin' to live with what happened, to find a strong woman inside her again. It'll take some time, and she could use a strong, decent man to help her do it. I ain't that man. You could be." He stepped up and ran a rough finger gently across the woman's cheek. "Goodbye, Maggie," he said softly.

Before she could respond, he was outside, mounted on his sorrel, and riding away, sadness settling on him like a tired man stretching out on a soft bed. He did not look back.

"This is the way it always is, Brodie Pike," he muttered. "You've brought enough trouble to that woman. Besides," he thought with a smile, "Little Raven would come back to haunt me for draggin' a town girl into the wilderness. She'd think me a savage." He laughed.

A Look At: Blood Trail
The Complete Western Series

Times were tough in the Old West, and Travis VanHorn can attest to that.

Humiliated and left to die by a band of ruthless outlaws, Travis VanHorn is saved by a man even harder than those who nearly killed him. From that moment on, Travis finds himself knee deep in suspenseful adventure.

The body count continues to rise, the stakes get higher and the battles get tougher. But Travis will follow the blood trail until the end – possibly his end.

The Blood Trail Series includes: Blood Trail, Blood Feud and Blood Vengeance.

AVAILABLE NOW

About the Author

John Legg has published more than 55 novels, all on Old West themes. Legg holds a B.A. in Communications and an M.S. in Journalism, and is a copy editor with The New York Times News Service.

Since his first two books, Legg has, under his own name, entertained the Western audience with many more tales of man's fight for independence on the Western frontier. In addition, he has had published several historical novels set in the Old West. Among those are WAR AT BENT'S FORT and BLOOD AT FORT BRIDGER.

In addition, Legg has, under pseudonyms, contributed to the RAMSEYS, a series that was published by Berkley, and was the sole author of the eight books in the SADDLE TRAMP series for HarperPaperbacks. He also was the sole author of WILDGUN, an eight-book adult Western series from Berkley/Jove.